THE WOUNDS OF THE DEAD

THE WOUNDS OF THE DEAD

Vikram Paralkar

4th

First published in India in 2017 by Fourth Estate
an imprint of HarperCollins *Publishers*

Building 10, Tower A, 4th Floor, DLF Cyber City, Phase II,
Gurugram Haryana – 122002, India
www.harpercollins.co.in

2 4 6 8 10 9 7 5 3 1

P-ISBN: 978-93-5277-437-1
E-ISBN: 978-93-5277-438-8

This is a work of fiction and all characters and incidents described in this book are the product of the author's imagination. Any resemblance to actual persons, living or dead, is entirely coincidental.

Typeset in Scala FF at
SURYA, New Delhi

Printed and bound at
MicroPrints India, New Delhi

One

The day the dead visited the surgeon, the air in his clinic was laced with formaldehyde. His pharmacist had poured some into a beaker in the operating room and given it a night to scour every corner. Once the door was opened, the acrid fumes spilled into the corridor and death leached out of the walls. This was the usual death, the mundane kind – that of insects and vermin.

~

The previous afternoon, a farmer had slit open the forearm of another with a sickle. They rushed up the hillock and crowded into the clinic, five farmers with a red trail behind them, holding the wound shut with a grimy rag.

The surgeon peeled off the cloth and saw the laceration from elbow to wrist.

'How did this happen?'

The injured man snarled through gritted teeth. 'This dog did it.'

Beside him, the accused hung his head. 'I was cutting

the grain, Doctor Saheb. I didn't see him bending down to pick up the bundle. Please stitch him up. I'll pay.'

The surgeon pressed the rag back onto the wound. 'It may not be so easy.' His pharmacist was standing by his side, ready with gloves on her hands. He passed the farmer's forearm over to her and let her lead the man to the operating room. The surgeon followed, stepping over the drops of blood in the man's wake. The other farmers stayed in the corridor. One of them pulled out a pouch of tobacco from his pocket.

'Don't spit on my walls,' warned the surgeon, and closed the door.

The pharmacist laid a drape over the stone slab of the operating table, and the surgeon asked the farmer to sit on a stool and stretch his arm across the cloth. He snapped on a pair of gloves and lifted the rag again. Blood oozed into the gash. The farmer puffed as the surgeon pulled the arm out straight along the length of the table.

The cut was long and irregular but shallow, confined to the skin for most of its length. The sickle had dug a little deeper in one place, but at least it hadn't nicked the artery. The sun was still up. There was enough light. The surgeon painted the skin brown with iodine and poured some into the wound itself, and with a piece of cotton soaked in alcohol, he traced the margin of the torn skin. The alcohol, as always, spread like oil on a lake, leaking into the cut. The farmer, who'd been biting his lip at the iodine, now threw his head back and started cursing someone's mother and sister.

'Enough,' the surgeon said. 'If you want me to do my work, you'll have to be quiet.'

'Saheb, the liquid burns.'

'Yes, I know. But it's necessary. And I'll tell you right now that I have very little numbing medicine – just two vials. I'll inject some of it here, but I won't be able to numb your whole arm. If you're shouting so much now, god knows what you'll do when it's time for the stitches.'

'I'll be quiet, Saheb.'

'And don't move your arm. Otherwise you can go to some other clinic and find another doctor to sew you up.'

The surgeon injected lidocaine into the edges of the wound and prepared his needle and suture while the numbing took effect. When he began stitching, the farmer bit down into his turban and whimpered, though without another word. And so it went.

Something scurried across the corner of the surgeon's vision. It was a cockroach at the base of the far wall, rustling its wings, curling and waving its antennae as though claiming the clinic for itself. The surgeon wanted to bellow at someone, but the pharmacist had stepped out to hand medicine to an old woman with a porous spine who visited the clinic every week with her unending complaints, and the farmer just sat there with his eyes clenched and his bloody arm extended before him. There was no one at whom the surgeon could holler: Why is there a filthy cockroach in my operating room? Am I supposed to play the exterminator around here as well? Mortar the cracks in the tiles? Pack the walls with poison?

The numbness in his fingers made the surgeon realize how hard he was gripping his forceps. He tried not to pour his anger into the needle and suture, but the more the cockroach scampered, the louder the farmer puffed into his turban. Then, after a stab that the surgeon himself thought regrettably brutal, the farmer gasped and raised his wet eyes. The surgeon slammed down his instruments and marched to the wall. The roach darted away. The surgeon stamped, but twice, thrice, it dodged him. Then he suspended his leg in the air, waited until the cockroach stopped running around and, when the moment was right, ground it under his heel. The rest of the suturing, he completed without interruption.

Just when he'd started to wonder if the pharmacist had fallen down a well, she returned to help him bandage the forearm. He wrote out a prescription for a tetanus vaccine and a course of antibiotics. The farmers outside the room had all left, except for one, who snapped up from his haunches as soon as the surgeon walked out into the corridor.

'You're the culprit, aren't you?'

'I'm sorry. I swear on my mother I didn't cut him on purpose. I didn't see—'

'Go buy these things from the city pharmacy. There should be a train leaving in fifteen minutes.'

'As you say, Doctor Saheb.' The man bowed and ran off.

The surgeon called the pharmacist, who'd left the operating room after bandaging the man's arm. 'Sterilize my instruments and fumigate the room.'

'Tonight?'

'Yes, tonight.'

'But, Saheb, there'll be children here tomorrow. For the polio drops.'

'Children? What do they have to do with this? There's a dead cockroach in there, and god knows how many live ones hiding in the walls. A cockroach in my operating room. What a disgrace. Only in *this* bloody clinic.'

~

The pharmacist winced as the door slammed in her face. Perhaps Saheb's back was troubling him again. She peeled away a fleck of rust from the edge of a metal tray and gathered the used instruments and the drape from the operating room on it. Saheb had clearly spent some energy in flattening the cockroach, and it took her some time to scrub its remains off the floor. A line of ants had already started to form, so she swept and mopped the rest of the room as well.

Then she taped shut every gap she could find in the windows, all the cracks in the frames, the spaces around their blunt, rounded corners. From the cabinet under the sink, she pulled out a large beaker and set it in the middle of the room. She poured the formalin halfway up to the black line – the clinic would be unbearable the next day if she filled it all the way. After confirming that she hadn't dropped anything in the room, especially not her mangalsutra, she added a few tablespoons of permanganate to the beaker. The mixture started bubbling, and she hurried out with the roll of tape and sealed the door behind her.

'What about the vaccines?' the surgeon called from his consultation room. 'Have they been delivered?'

'No, not yet, Saheb. They were going to come today.'

'Then what are we supposed to do for the polio drive? Spray the children with rosewater? Worthless, all of them. Some lazy official must have spent the day eating mutton at his aunt's place instead of delivering the cases. If he isn't here by tomorrow morning, I swear I'll file complaints in the head office every week till they fire him.'

He emerged, the newspaper rolled in his hand like a policeman's club. 'I'm going. If patients come for me and they aren't dying, tell them to return tomorrow.'

'Yes, Saheb.'

~

A full bladder pulled the surgeon from sleep, and the rattle of the ceiling fan kept him from returning to it. The fan wasn't loud, but it had a maddening rhythm, a monotonous, creaking pulse. He thought about prisoners who'd reportedly lost their sanity after enduring such things – dripping water and the like. Who knew if those tales were even true? At this hour, they sounded plausible.

It was almost exactly three years since he'd come to this place. Three years in these rooms, in the tiny quarters adjoining the clinic. The windows were just as they'd been when he arrived, actually a little worse now, their squares of mosquito netting perforated by the constant pecking of sparrows. And what protection had the netting provided him against that bout of dengue anyway? The illness had come and gone, but it had left a fatigue that still lingered all these months on. He sometimes wondered if the disease hadn't affected his brain as well. When he first moved here, he'd resolved never to let his mind stagnate, no matter how bad things got. He'd brought his library with him, three tall bookcases to surround his bed, his bulwarks against this unlettered village. When was the last time he'd taken a book from the shelves? The tomes were just chunks of yellow paper now, collections of purposeless sentences trailing each other from cover to cover for no good reason.

These menial chores – draining abscesses, treating coughs and diarrhoea, extracting rotten teeth, and now, another great feat, squashing cockroaches. All for what? To live in this hovel?

He could walk across the room and turn the creaking fan off, but the effort didn't seem worth it. Sleep wouldn't come either way. He cradled the back of his head in his fingers and watched the blades chase each other in grey circles.

~

At dawn, the pharmacist strapped on a surgical mask and stepped into the eye-watering cloud of formaldehyde engulfing the clinic. She threw open every window, even set out small bowls of ammonia in each of the four rooms, but the fumes wouldn't dissipate. She tried to switch on a fan.

The run back home left her too breathless to get her words out.

'Wake up, wake up. The clinic lights aren't working. The fridge is warming up. Doctor Saheb will be so angry.'

Her husband looked barely conscious as she dragged him up the hillock, but the noxious fog at the top blew the sleep right out of him. She didn't want to torture him like this, but who else in the village knew the clinic's wiring?

'The fuses,' he said. 'Third time this month.'

She let him grumble. With his red eyes, his uncombed hair, and the handkerchief tied across his nose and mouth, he could have been mistaken for a bandit. He pushed a ladder up against the door of the operating room and climbed to the electrical box. When he opened it, even she, from where she stood, could see black moustaches on either side of the fuse beds – remnants of repeated burnings.

'Give me the screwdriver. And that wire.'

She dug in the box. 'Can't you do something to stop it burning again?'

'I'll talk to Saheb about this machine, a "surhjagard", they call it, I think. I've never seen one. It's expensive. And I'll have to change a lot of wiring to make it all go through one line.'

'Don't talk about it today, then. It's going to be a bad day, I know it.'

He unscrewed the wrong connection at first, then tightened it again, then coughed until she was afraid he would fall off the ladder. Every few minutes he leaned down, and she wiped his eyes with the same cloth with which she was wiping her own. Finally, he twisted the last copper wires together, and when he pressed the fuses into place and turned the switch, the lights, the fans, the refrigerator, all began to hum and creak.

As he was putting the ladder away, Saheb walked up the steps. 'What happened? Why are you crying?'

'Not crying, Saheb. Just the fumigation.'

These fumes never seemed to bother Saheb. Maybe it was part of his training all those years ago. That, and the cutting open of corpses, the pharmacist had heard. Doctors were brave people. She would die if she ever had to watch something like that.

Saheb went to his chair. 'Have the vaccines arrived?'

'No, not yet.' She tried to retie the straps on her mask, but it was too large for her face.

'What are those rascals doing? Did anyone call to explain the delay?'

'I tried, but no one picked up the phone.'

'Fine. If that's the way it's going to be, I don't care. It's not my vaccine drive anyway. What do I have to lose?'

Over the next hours, the mothers started arriving. They squatted on the grass at a distance, covered their faces and fanned their children. If it hadn't been for the fumes, they would have crowded into the corridor and piled on the benches in twos and threes. Perhaps it was a blessing they weren't doing that now. Not even a week had passed since the pharmacist's husband had hammered the planks back together.

For the past few days, the tiny television in the village square had been broadcasting the same public service announcement on the Marathi channel – round-faced mothers in saris and burkhas smiling and holding hands while a deep, kind voice said, 'Give your babies a gift. Protect their futures. Just two pink drops.' Then a child's sweet face – one that always made the pharmacist's eyes fill – would appear. She knew what would come next: the shrunken leg, the crutch in the armpit, the sunset. 'Make sure you come,' she'd said to every woman she'd met. 'Early in the morning. Tell everyone.'

Now it seemed that ten villages' worth of mothers had taken her advice. And the vaccines seemed more likely to rain from the sky than be delivered.

She closed the pharmacy window and started rearranging shelves that didn't really need her attention. When the day crept past noon, she avoided the eyes of the complaining crowd as she carried lunch and ice water to the surgeon.

He placed a tablet on his tongue and gulped it down. 'Look, if the man doesn't show up in another half an hour, send the women away. If they start yelling, tell them to march to the district office and set up a hunger strike there. Just tell them not to bother me. I don't brew vaccines in my kitchen. Understood?'

'Yes, Saheb.'

'And tell them all to be quiet. My head is going to explode. Let me at least have a peaceful meal.'

'Yes, Saheb.'

~

The surgeon was polishing the last morsels off his plate when the pharmacist's husband knocked.

'He's here.'

The surgeon looked out of the window. A corpulent shape in a faded blue safari jacket was puffing up the hillock. The man had an exuberant moustache and square glasses, and was carrying six large thermocol boxes. The sea of squatting women parted to let him pass.

The surgeon washed his hands and stepped into the corridor, every ounce of his flesh already pickled with contempt. The visitor laid down his load.

'Here are the vaccines.'

'You were supposed to bring these yesterday.'

'I was delayed.'

'That's it? You were delayed? And what about us? Are we beggars, waiting for you to throw us alms?'

The official looked at the women who had hurried into the corridor after him, and who were now tugging at the corners of their saris, veiling their faces against his eyes.

'It's no business of yours why I'm late. I'm here now, am I not?'

'Not a shred of responsibility. Is this what you're paid to do? Every other day is a vacation for you people. Who gives a damn about the doctor? For all you care, he can get holy water from the Ganga and drip it down his villagers' throats.'

'Don't raise your voice, Saheb. I'm not some peon.'

'You think I'm scared of you?'

'I've been placed in charge of this village, this clinic.

I'm your supervisor. You don't want to get into trouble with me.'

'Really? What kind of trouble?'

The official rubbed his moustache and then inspected his fingers as if afraid he'd find them stained with dye. 'I didn't want to bring this up here, in front of all these people, but there have been irregularities reported in this clinic. Questions about how your money is spent.'

The surgeon packed as much derision as he could into his laugh. 'You mean the money that doesn't even *reach* us? The money that turns to smoke the moment you and your comrades touch it?'

'Saheb, look, you have vaccines to give out. Why are you wasting time with this kind of talk?'

'Don't teach me how to do my work. I would have been dispensing them since eight if you hadn't been so lazy. But now that you've brought up irregularities, let's talk about irregularities. Just wait. I'll make sure you learn every financial detail about this clinic.'

He gripped the official's arm, digging his thumb and fingers deep into the man's biceps. The man's eyes widened. The surgeon strode into the consultation room, dragging the official in with him, and then released him with enough force to make him fall into a chair. The glass door of the wall cabinet gave a piercing rasp as the surgeon slid it aside, and he yanked out his tattered moss-green ledger and slammed it on the desk.

'Here's my account book. Pay particular attention to this section, page fifty-two onwards, where I've listed the amounts I've had to spend from my own pocket to keep this place from turning into an archaeological ruin. *That's* an irregularity worth noting, isn't it?'

The official sat as if every part of him, down to his fingers, were welded to the chair.

'I've been working here without a nurse. I've asked the head office to budget me one, to issue advertisements in the district newspaper, but no, my application's been pending in your office for months. I need a new autoclave machine – the old pressure drum we have could blow up in our faces any minute. I need an EKG machine, a suction unit for the operating room ... No one can run a clinic like this. A morgue perhaps, not a clinic. Every month I have to spend my own salary to keep this place together. I buy antibiotics and sutures. And kerosene for the generator. I know how much money is assigned to this clinic in the government budget, but you middlemen eat it up, you fat pigs. Sit here, sit with this ledger. Conduct your investigation. Prepare a detailed report for your superiors. I'll wait.'

The look on the official's jowly face was the most satisfying thing the surgeon had seen in months. As if he were thawing himself out of a block of ice, the man started tapping his fingers and making grinding sounds with his teeth. A woman in the crowd behind him giggled. The official scowled, pulled a small booklet out of his pocket and compared some scribblings in it to the numbers in the ledger. A few times he made as if to write something, but his pen never actually touched paper. Finally, the formaldehyde seemed to get the best of him, and he pressed a handkerchief to his nose.

'I'll need to look around the clinic.'

'Look all you want. It's just four rooms, so take as long as you need. Do you require a magnifying glass?'

The official turned and went into the corridor. The women moved aside as they might have for a serpent.

The surgeon snorted. This one was a novice. The experts among his kind knew how to play their hands with more skill. They knew how to sniff out the naïvely dishonest; erode confidence with pointed observations, ominous frowns, knowing *hmms* and *tsks*; apply the slow, escalated pressure that they'd all learnt from their bastard supervisors, who'd learnt it from the endless hierarchy of bastard supervisors above them. Once the prey was cowed enough to reveal some slight indiscretion, some minor misuse of government funds for personal gain, the bastard's work was done. He could then put his feet up and recite his lines: 'Never mind, never mind, everyone makes mistakes. A single mistake doesn't make you a bad person. Of course the government is very strict about its rules. It has a responsibility to the public. But I would never wish your reputation to be soiled. Perhaps we can reach an arrangement. Seal everything within these four walls.'

The seas would boil before he'd tolerate such nonsense in his clinic.

While the surgeon was unpacking boxes and arranging vaccines in the refrigerator, someone pointed at the window. He looked up to see the official worming his way out through the crowd. The surgeon cupped his hands around his mouth and shouted, 'Next time forget the vaccines. Just bring us some water from the Ganga.'

The safari jacket receded at a faster pace.

~

If only the day could have ended there. But now there were these women. The hillock was crawling with their offspring.

The pharmacist's husband stood in the corridor like a traffic guard, organizing the crowd into queues, directing them either to the surgeon or the pharmacist.

The surgeon squeezed two pink drops onto an infant's tongue. It coughed and burst into a wail, the vaccine bubbling on its lips in pink spittle, and its mother gathered it up on her shoulder and patted it.

'Done. Next.'

'Thank you, Doctor Saheb. Your blessings on my daughter.'

'Come on, come on. Next. What am I, a priest? There are other people waiting.'

The young mother, barely more than a girl herself, was replaced by another who could well have been her twin, for all he knew. This one had a three-year-old in a shabby brown tunic. He was rubbing his eyes and mewling.

'My eyes hurt.'

'I know, I know.' She was trying to hold him steady. 'Just take this medicine and we'll go.'

'But it's burning. My eyes are burning.'

'Saheb is waiting, my child.' She tried to pry the little mouth open, but the boy squirmed, twisted his head this way and that.

The surgeon clenched his jaw. Who did they think they were? They could take the vaccine or get out, it was nothing to him either way. What did they know of his qualifications? Of his skills? He was glad the fumes were burning their eyes, the eyes of their brats too, so they could know that he was a surgeon and not some village quack. He hoped their eyes would burn all the more with that knowledge.

He said little else as the chain of mothers and children trickled through the clinic. The afternoon passed, and the assembly on the hillock thinned.

~

After the last of them had left, and the formaldehyde had wrung out all the tears it could and drifted away, the surgeon sank into his chair. The sun was a bag of blood sliced open by the horizon, smearing the squat brick houses. The parched ground stretched before him, covered with a rash of dry yellow weed.

Every speck of this village seemed created to crush the life out of him. He felt an intense hatred for it all – the dust that lay heavy on the earth, the bone-white trees clawing with ludicrous ambition at the sky, even the mongrels that limped from door to door for scraps of meat. If it could all vanish, the world would only be enriched.

He faced the window and ran his fingers through his hair – what little was left of it – as the sun extinguished itself on the huts in the distance and darkness dripped like pitch over the dreary village. 'No more.' He yawned. 'No more.' From this day on, not a paisa of his own money would be spent on this place. Whatever savings he had, he would gather them and leave. Two months at the most while he arranged for a house somewhere. Anywhere. The official could take this bloody clinic and turn it into a tomb.

Two

The surgeon, his head buried in a ledger, was adding a long string of numbers when someone said, 'Doctor Saheb.'

The nib of his pen halted, and he watched an inky halo blossom around it and spread through the cheap paper. The calculations in his mind evaporated. He looked up.

There were visitors in his doorway. He hadn't heard them step into the clinic.

'The polio drive is over. The vaccines are all finished. Nothing left.'

With his pen, the surgeon pointed at the boy, an oval-faced child with untidy hair sticking out behind his ears. 'How old is your son?'

'Eight,' replied the man.

'Then he doesn't need this vaccine. It's only for children five years and younger.'

'We aren't here for the vaccine, Doctor Saheb.'

Fingerprints smudged the surgeon's bifocals, and he had to pick them off his nose and wipe them clean to take a better look. He couldn't remember having seen these people before. The man was slim, his face oval like his son's, but stubbled. The woman standing behind the boy was perhaps a little younger than the man. Probably the wife. Her odhni was wrapped so strangely around her neck and chin that he couldn't see a mangalsutra.

'What is it, then?' the surgeon asked, returning to his ledger. First the encounter with the official, then his confinement in this room, monotonously forcing drops into bawling children – it had ground him down to his marrow. And then there was his misplaced perfectionism, his inability to fill the vaccine ledger with meaningless scribbles and be done with it. The ledgers would be filed away in some government archive and never opened again, but still he needed the serial numbers on the invoices to match the boxes, the boxes to match the aliquots, the aliquots to tally with groups of children. And he was almost done. Fifteen minutes without interruption – that was all he needed.

What the hell was the pharmacist doing, anyway? Last he knew, she was in the storeroom, folding cardboard boxes to line the medicine cabinets. Instead of doing her origami, that girl should have stopped these three at the front steps. 'It's late,' she should have said. 'The clinic is closed. Come back tomorrow.'

But she was nowhere in sight. He would have to deal with them himself.

'Are you deaf? What do you want?'

The visitors flinched. 'We need your help,' the man said. 'This will seem like a strange request.'

'Strange request? What nonsense is this? Just state your business or get going.'

Now, finally, the pharmacist rushed in, panicked. 'What are you doing here? You can't disturb Saheb like this. Wait outside, wait outside.' She began to usher them out.

But when the boy moved aside, the surgeon noticed the bulge under the woman's loose clothing. He raised his hand.

'Is your wife in labour? Did her water break?'

'No. She's almost at term, as you can see, but that's not why we're here. Or at least, not just that.'

The man paused, rubbed his mouth with the back of his palm. His eyelids parted farther, and he stammered out his next words.

'We-we're seriously injured. All three of us. And we need surgeries. Tonight.'

The visitor clearly wasn't a bumpkin. He was educated – his choice of words left no doubt about that. But surgeries? Had the surgeon heard him right? What could the man possibly—

'Show me,' said the surgeon.

Like merchants displaying their wares, the boy rolled up his vest and the man unbuttoned his shirt and lifted his right arm over his head. In the man's side was a slit, its edges white and still, like lips paused in speech. It was enough to fool one into thinking that the ribs had been penetrated. The boy's abdomen was bloated. Two cuts in the upper left, under the ribcage, formed a cross whose corners curled outward. And then the woman finished peeling away the many loops of odhni wrapped around her neck. It couldn't be. He had to be mistaken. The wound in her neck – surely it was a trick of the light? Could those be the ends of her muscles? And was that – no, it was impossible – the *larynx*?

But there was no blood gushing out, not even from that neck. What kind of hoax was this? Who were these charlatans?

Out of the corner of his eye, the surgeon saw a jerking motion. It was the pharmacist. The surgeon had forgotten that she was still in the room. She looked rigid, as though in the grip of a seizure. The man with the cut in his side sprang to her and grabbed both her wrists with one hand. Stepping behind her, he clapped his other hand over her mouth. She was thin, but seemed to match him in strength as they struggled. He grimaced as he twisted her forearms and muscled her to him, her back against his chest, her torso immobilized by the pressure of his arm folded across her, locking her twitching hands against his shoulder.

The air seemed to clot, grow viscous. The surgeon pushed through it, tried to reach the pharmacist. He felt his books fly off the desk as his hand struck them. The woman with the monstrous neck blocked his path, clasped his wrist, pressed a finger to her lips.

'Please, Doctor Saheb, please,' the man said. 'I won't hurt her, won't hurt you. We are good people. We just need your help.'

'What—' the surgeon began, but could find no suitable words to add. So he just stood and watched – watched the man signal the boy; watched the boy run to the window, close and latch it, bolt the door; watched the woman go to the pharmacist and reach out to cup her cheek, all the while speaking rapidly, calling her 'sister', begging her not to scream.

This was no hoax. The pharmacist, twisting in her captor's grip, arched her body back like a bow at the woman's advance, making the man stumble a step back to maintain his hold on her. The girl's eyelids had opened as far as they could go, and her eyes were fixed on the woman's obscene neck. The surgeon felt his own muscles knot and pull at the point where the nerves threaded out from his skull. He pressed his hand on the cold glass plate of the desk behind him.

The man with the cut in his ribs opened his mouth, but if he said something, the surgeon could not hear it. The woman fell quiet and, probably realizing the effect her injuries were having, raised her odhni and let it drape back around her neck, removing her wound from view.

The surgeon's eyes darted around the room. Could he use his pen as a weapon, was it sharp enough, solid enough? It lay on the floor, its nib snapped off. A spray of ink stretched across the tiles. What else? He had scissors in his drawer somewhere, he was sure, but he'd have to dig for them.

He gripped the table's edge tighter, leaned against it. 'What is this? What's going on?'

The visitors stood like effigies. The woman and the boy turned to the man, who was opening and closing his mouth like a fish thrown to land. The girl he held captive had stopped her struggle and now just hung against him, breathing heavily with her eyes squeezed shut. He too closed his eyes and heaved, as though gathering his breath for some feat.

'I'm a teacher, Doctor Saheb. This is my family. We've never harmed anyone. We just want to live our lives in peace.'

Three

'We'd gone to a fair near our village,' said the man who called himself a teacher. 'It was sunset by the time we left it. The street was dark. The bulbs in the lamp posts had burned out. I didn't think much of it then, didn't turn back. God knows how much I've repented that.'

The pharmacist started squirming again in the man's grip. His words spilled out faster.

'Four men were hiding there. They jumped out, took our money and jewellery. And then they stabbed us, Doctor Saheb, stabbed us and left us on the roadside. Like sacks of garbage. They just left us there and disappeared.'

The visitors were pale. There was a sickly tone to their skin, that was true. But how—

'When did this happen?' the surgeon asked.

'This evening.'

'But, but there was no fair here. I didn't hear of any—'

'It didn't happen here, Saheb. We're from another district.'

'But that doesn't make any sense. How did you get here? The sun just set, not even an hour ago. And how did you stop your bleeding?'

'We didn't.'

The surgeon felt his toes curl in his shoes, press hard against the leather. 'But then how did you survive?'

'We didn't.'

This was unacceptable. One could string letters together to say anything, anything at all, no matter how outrageous. The surgeon wished his thoughts would connect, one to the next, turn the man's words into something that made sense.

He took a step towards the family. The teacher's wife, as if she'd read his mind, lowered the odhni and tilted her neck away, letting her wound gape. The sight was suffocating, and the surgeon staggered back and collapsed into a chair as his legs gave under him. How was one to shake off such a hallucination? Perhaps he ought to bash his head against something – the desk, the wall ... fracture his skull if need be. Would that do it?

The silence felt like an awful pressure on his eardrums. His eyes kept flitting to the drawer, the one that supposedly had scissors in it. At one point, he heard a sob, and it took him some time to realize it was the pharmacist. She was hanging limp in the teacher's hold.

The surgeon sat up in his chair. 'Let her go.'

'I—I can't, Doctor Saheb. She'll wake up the villagers. I can't let that happen.'

'She'll be quiet. Let her go.'

The teacher turned to his wife with an anxious look, then pinched shut his eyes and loosened his grip. The girl tore away from him and flung herself into the farthest corner of the room. There she whimpered, high and soft, but did not scream.

The surgeon leaned forward, pressed his thumbs hard into his eyelids. Webs and vortices danced in the darkness.

'We need you, Doctor Saheb. There's no one else.'

'What are you saying? What are you—'

'Without your help we will remain dead.'

'The dead do not walk,' said the surgeon, his head reeling with vertigo. 'The dead do not speak. The dead have no choice but to remain dead. You are lying to me.'

'I understand what you're feeling, Saheb, believe me. If I were in your place, I would have found this as impossible as you do. When I was alive, I never believed stories of ghosts and possessions and haunted houses – the tales that old men told their grandchildren to scare them. All nonsense, I knew. I always taught my students to reject superstition. You have no reason to trust my words, Doctor Saheb, I understand that. But trust our wounds. Examine them, and then tell me. Who could stay alive with injuries like ours?'

The surgeon released the pressure on his eyes. The vortices spun away and vanished, but the family remained, shrouded by a haze as though their bodies were fraying at the edges, unravelling. He couldn't will them out of existence. Every blink of his eyes brought the family more into focus, made them more solid.

'Look, are you a thief of some kind? Just say so if you are. I have money in my safe. Take it and go. You don't need to do this elaborate—'

'Please, Doctor Saheb, please listen. At dawn, we will live again.'

It couldn't be. It just couldn't. 'Why have you come to me? Go find a priest, a sorcerer. Leave me alone.'

'We need you to fix our wounds. At sunrise, our bodies will fill with blood again, and we'll no longer be walking corpses.'

'How? Why? How is that possible?'

'The answer is long and complicated, Saheb, and I don't understand everything myself. I can only tell you now that an angel took mercy on us. I'll explain everything else later. We have so little time. I know nothing about surgeries, but I'm sure that injuries as severe as ours will take you all night to stitch up.'

The surgeon's chest felt cold, tight. 'Are you mad? You want me to operate on you here? In *this* clinic? I don't even have instruments to set a fracture, let alone repair torn blood vessels and whatever internal injuries you have. Whatever this is, this insanity, it can't be done here. You must go to the city. Go.'

'But, Doctor Saheb—'

'There's a train that leaves every hour. It will take you there.'

'Saheb—'

'Maybe the train isn't a good idea. You can drive there. Here, take my car. I don't care, you don't even have to bring it back. Can you drive? No? Okay, then, I'll drive you. I'll drop you off at a proper hospital. You can explain everything to the doctors there, get them to treat you.'

He went to the pharmacist. She was pressed to the wall, as though trying to percolate to the other side.

'Come.' He helped her up, began to steer her to the door.

'Wait,' said the teacher. He looked desperate. 'We can't go to the city. Whatever you can do here, in this clinic, is all we're allowed. If we even step beyond the boundary of this village, the angel will snatch our lives back.'

'What? But that doesn't make any sense. Why would angels care about village boundaries?'

'I swear to you, Saheb, it's the truth. It was his most important condition.'

'But that's just ridiculous. You must have heard him wrong. Look, I'll just drop this girl off with her husband and get my car ready. Let's not waste time.'

He was almost at the door, reaching for the bolt, when the teacher spoke, so softly that even a breeze might have swept his voice away. 'If we were to drive with you, Saheb, our bodies would stop moving at the boundary, and you would be left with three corpses to keep you company for the rest of your journey.'

The surgeon jerked to a stop. Something settled in his skull, dense as lead, a sudden condensation of all the grotesquerie of this evening. He could already imagine the family on his operating table, lying there as he worked on their bloodless flesh, corpses laid upon stone slabs in preparation for autopsies – his mind rebelled against that word, but what other name could one give to surgeries on the dead? This night contained nothing but absurdities.

'Have mercy on us,' the teacher was saying. 'If our wounds aren't closed, we'll die another death, as bloody and horrible as the first. If you can't do anything for me, at least help my wife and son. Give life to them, to my unborn child, I beg you. I have nothing on me, no money, but I'll do anything you ask. Just don't turn us away.'

The man threw himself at the surgeon's feet. The doctor stood like an imbecile, unable even to recoil from the dead fingers clutching his shoes, able only to repeat, 'No, no, don't do that, don't do that.'

Four

'Wait here, in this room. I need some time,' said the surgeon to the dead as he helped the pharmacist out into the corridor. She hung from him like a dead weight, her face so grey that he thought she would faint any moment.

He closed the door behind him and set her down on a bench, propped against the wall. After raising her lids with a thumb against her eyebrows to confirm that there was life still there, he sank beside her.

To be freed, even for a moment, from the dead and the dreadful hope in their eyes was an intense relief. The breeze wafting in through the entrance of the clinic was warm, and outside the shuttered room, no longer faced with bloodless wounds, he could once again breathe. Far below, oil lamps flickered in the windows of the village at the bottom of the hill. Behind those windows, the villagers were probably washing dishes, tossing leftovers out for the crows, dousing embers, unrolling mattresses. As though this night were no different from any other. As though it were obvious that the sun would rise again.

The girl was whimpering. The surgeon knew that something was required of him, consoling words perhaps, but all he could do was grip his kneecaps. It was the only way he could still the shaking of his hands. There would be no one to console him – it was best he accepted that first.

'This is just ... just so impossible,' he said. 'I don't know what to think.'

The girl swallowed, then coughed, choking on her tears. 'They're ghosts, Saheb.' She could barely get the words out past her chattering teeth.

Something rustled outside the entrance, and even though the surgeon could tell it was only a rat in the grass, the muscles in his arms and shoulders tightened. The pharmacist didn't even notice. The effort of speaking seemed too much for her.

'A ghost climbed into my sister's body, Saheb. We had to tie her to a bed. She kept turning, one side to the other, kicked at everyone. Said things, Saheb, that no one could understand. Her eyes, they were rolled up; her body became hot, like burning coal – so hot that no one could touch her. And her mouth was full of foam, as if she'd eaten soap.'

The girl had never mentioned her sister before. Would he have remembered if she had?

'My father, he called a tantrik. Told him to do whatever magic he could to save her. The tantrik had to beat her with a broom to drive the ghost out – that's how tightly it held her, like a crab. On the third day, it left her body and went into a coconut. The tantrik broke it open and blood spilled out. So much blood, I thought I would die. My sister woke up, but she didn't recognize any of us.'

'How long ago was this?'

'Six years. No, more. Eight. She lived, but what kind of life is this? The ghost made her mind weak. She can't even feed herself. My mother still has to change her clothes every day. No one will marry her.'

The surgeon had witnessed spectacles such as this before – charlatans with hair that had seen neither comb nor water in god knew how long, wearing bone necklaces around their necks, jumping and chanting to Goddess Kali and spraying so much red water around that the room looked washed with blood. The trickery was always so transparent, but the gullible believed what they wanted to believe. A few days of antibiotics would have done the poor girl more good than a lifetime of holy water and chants.

But it was hard to dismiss ghosts so glibly now, with three of them waiting on the other side of the wall.

'We have to run away, Saheb. We have to leave the village before something bad happens.'

The clock in front of them had only one hand. No, there were two, overlapping between eight and nine. A small green lizard was pasted to the wall next to the clock, as still as its hands.

'If the man had wanted to strangle you,' said the surgeon, 'he would've just done it. He already had his hand around your mouth. There was nothing to stop him.'

With a click, one hand of the clock stepped out from behind the other. The lizard slithered off to the wall's edge.

If even a word of what the dead had said was true, they couldn't just sit here and keep talking like this.

'Their wounds need to be repaired. I don't know how I'm going to do it, but they need to be repaired.'

From the look on the pharmacist's face, he might have been speaking a foreign tongue.

'Look, either we help them, or they die. Die again, that is – however you want to think about it. It's not a question of whether any of this makes sense. It's a question of ... of whether we're going to just kick them out of the clinic or not. And if not, we have to do something.'

Her eyes had already begun to widen. It was clear she knew what he would say next. So he said it.

'I'll need your help for this.'

'Me? No, Doctor Saheb, no,' she almost screamed.

'Quiet. We have to be quiet.'

She dropped her voice, which only made her sound more hoarse. 'What are you saying, Saheb? I can't stay here. I can't. This is not right. These things shouldn't happen, it's not right, it's not right.'

He leaned against the wall. Whatever he was feeling now – the fear and fatigue – the night would only magnify it. Perhaps her instinct was the right one. Perhaps he should just leap into his car and drive away in any direction, abandon the village and everything in it. In the morning, the villagers would find three cadavers in the clinic. Or the visitors, recognizing the idiocy of their plan, would decide to walk to the boundary of the village and fall there. Either was infinitely preferable to his involvement in this dreadful matter, the raising, no, the mending of the dead.

'You've always done everything I've asked,' he said. 'If you want to leave, I won't stop you. Maybe if things were any different, I would have left as well. But the woman is pregnant. Her son is just eight. We have to do something.'

At first it seemed as if she hadn't heard him, but then her face turned to the ground and her chest began to shake. The way her braid hung between her bony shoulders made her look more like a child than ever. He thought of placing a hand on her head, but couldn't bring himself to do so, not even at a time like this. 'It will be fine,' was all he managed to say, his hands still on his knees. 'It will be fine.'

But he couldn't ask her not to weep. As the lights in the village winked out one by one, he tried to push away his own disquiet while he waited, but it was like trying to sweep a fog aside with his fingers. Whatever this was, this inescapable madness, he would have to get through it. He would pretend that the visitors had been wheeled in on gurneys, with lolling heads and frothing mouths, victims of some mysterious accident. He would just do his job, and let the pieces fall as they would.

The girl finally wiped her face. Taking that as a sign, he stood up.

'Your husband must be wondering where you are. I'll need his help as well. Let me explain everything. And we have to be careful. If the villagers hear about this, they'll bring down the sky.'

Five

The lights in the operating room flickered on. The faintest trace of formaldehyde still hung in the air. Glazed tiles with bluish veins covered the walls to a height of four feet. Many were chipped and broken. Despite the pharmacist's regular scrubbing, grime had settled into the grout, and the paint on the wall above, once a shiny white, was now blistered with green geographies of mould.

A loop of sturdy metal hung from the plastered ceiling. The large tungsten reflector lamp that was intended to hang from it had never been delivered, vanishing, like so many things, into the bureaucratic ether. The room was lit instead by a fluorescent tube mounted high on one of the walls, and by two tall anglepoise lamps that the surgeon had himself purchased. Together they cast a modest illumination, suitable for minor procedures like the suturing of shallow cuts or the extraction of glass shards, but certainly not for any real surgery. Only a lunatic would suggest doing anything here in the middle of the night.

These last few years, the surgeon had wondered if he had the right to operate at all any more. With a well-lit surgical field, he might still have trusted his skills. But in this room, where lamps cast shadows, concealing more than they exposed, every nerve or blood vessel or loop of bowel could hide in a dark corner and conspire to brush against his scalpel's edge. It was impossible to operate safely here. Inflamed appendices, gall bladders, bowel obstructions – he sent them all to the city hospitals. What did he have to offer anyway? No nurse, no blood bank, no light. If a patient had to die, she would die from her disease, not from his surgery.

A glass cabinet on the wall housed his instruments – relics of his past. It was the pharmacist's job to keep them sterilized and bundled in thick green cloth. Their shine was rarely marred by use. The surgeon would just unwrap the green wombs and sort through his collection, arrange his tools by size and type, hold them up to the light one by one as though approving them for a surgery, until he could no longer ignore the absurdity of this farce.

'These need to be autoclaved,' he would say, and drop them back on the tray.

'Yes, Saheb.'

The instruments were sterilized far more often than they were used, but the pharmacist never complained. She would just wrap them back in the squares of cloth, pack them into fenestrated metal boxes, set them in the autoclave drum, and wait while the machine steamed and whistled. Then she would extract the contents with sterile gloves and stack them back in the glass cabinet until the surgeon felt the need to inspect them again. Because of this pointless routine, all the instruments in the cabinet were always ready for surgery. And they were ready now.

Still, it was just a humble set of implements – basic tools for mundane surgeries, nothing very specialized. The dead seemed to think him a magician, with mystical devices and superhuman powers. How many disappointments was he destined to inflict on them?

And what agonies? The surgeon had worried about this since the beginning. Would they feel pain? He had no equipment for anaesthesia – no propofol, no thiopental. And even if he did, how could the drugs work on the dead without a bloodstream? He might have to crack their chests open without the basic luxury of lowering them into slumber. Did they understand that?

To these concerns, the teacher said, 'Our wounds don't hurt. We don't even feel them. It's part of our state. We won't feel any pain for the rest of this night.'

'And what about tomorrow morning?'

'We'll have life and blood at dawn, Saheb, so I assume we'll also have pain. When that happens, we will endure it. We'll endure whatever we have to.'

~

The surgeon knocked on the door of the pharmacist's house. The pharmacist stood at his side, wringing her hands as though trying to scrub them clean of some unseen stain.

Her husband opened the door. 'What is it, Saheb? You here? At this time? Is there a problem?'

'Yes, a problem. You could call it that.'

'Go get Saheb a glass of water,' the man said to his wife, but his eyes didn't leave the surgeon.

'No need for water.' The surgeon waved his hand. 'This will seem like a strange request.' It struck him, after he'd spoken, that these were the same words with which the dead had begun explaining their predicament.

'Saheb?'

'Walk up the hill with me.'

The clinic sat on the hillock like a lantern. They walked in silence past the houses and huts of the village, and then, once they had started climbing, the surgeon spoke in slow, careful words, some of which he had to dig out of a vocabulary he'd never dreamed he'd use. The windows of the clinic seemed to grow brighter with every step. The moon had not risen, and it was as though the foot of the hillock were the rim of the world, with only nothingness beyond it. When they reached the top, the surgeon found himself short of breath, as if he'd hiked a great distance, and he stopped speaking.

A few yards from the entrance, the pharmacist's husband squatted on his heels and slapped his hands to his cheeks. A string of fearful questions poured out of his mouth. What good could possibly come of this? The only reason ghosts ever came back was to harass the living. What if they wanted to possess them all? Haunt them and drive them mad? Maybe even kill them?

The surgeon, exhausted by his own incomprehension, offered answers that barely convinced even himself. What right had he to the allegiances of these two? It humiliated him to be placed in this position, but how else would he get through the night? The pharmacist just knelt at her husband's side and avoided the surgeon's eyes.

The man would run, and he would take her with him, the surgeon felt sure. It was futile to hope for anything different. And why indeed should the man not do as he wished? If corpses could walk, what remained to guide any other action?

A silhouette moved in the clinic's light. The teacher's son was leaning against the entrance. With the bulb at his back, his outline threw a long shadow across the bright strip that stretched from the clinic door, out over the grass. Behind everything was the sky – an inky spread with pinpricks of white. When the surgeon's eyes met his, the boy inched back into the corridor, and his face fell in the bulb's light. He looked guilty, as if he knew he didn't belong there, in this place and this world. The boy's parents appeared behind him. 'What are you doing here? Saheb told us to wait inside,' said the teacher. He cast a nervous glance at the pharmacist's husband, then at the surgeon, and began to lead his son away, but the surgeon gestured for them to stay.

The pharmacist clutched her husband's arm. 'There they are, there they are.'

'Yes, there they are,' said the surgeon. 'The dead. They're here to regain their own lives, not to steal yours.'

The pharmacist's husband slumped back. He rubbed his eyes, stared, rubbed them again, trying perhaps, as the surgeon had tried not that long ago, to scrub away the hallucination. The surgeon himself, observing the dead for the first time from outside his clinic, was struck by how like the living they looked, standing there surrounded by bulbs and benches and discoloured paint, as though the corridor were the place where all the entities of this world and the next could blend together seamlessly. Nothing more than a doorframe separated the dead from the living now, and who could say in that moment who stood on which side?

The pharmacist rose, helped her husband up. The surgeon looked away, tried not to eavesdrop as they murmured to each other. Nothing he could say would accomplish more than the sight of the dead themselves.

'If you think this has to be done,' said the pharmacist's husband, his lips a dull white, 'we trust you.'

'If you want to leave, go now.'

'You have done more for us, for the villagers, than anyone else, Saheb. We are in your debt.'

'If you want to go, I understand,' repeated the surgeon, perversely hoping they would take the opportunity to fly. 'Really, I understand.'

'We can't leave you here. We'll do whatever you tell us. The rest is in god's hands.'

The surgeon nodded. It was the most he could manage by way of gratitude. His face felt permanently carved in a grave expression of foreboding. He turned and made for the clinic.

The teacher came up to him at the steps. 'I was wondering, Saheb, if you think it's wise to involve more people in this. The fewer who know, the better, don't you think?'

'There won't be any more,' said the surgeon. 'And without these two to help me, you might as well prepare for your second death.'

Responsible now for both the living and the dead, he dragged himself up into the corridor. The teacher appeared to have more to say, but the surgeon was in no mood to hear it.

Six

'Keep watch here,' the surgeon said to the pharmacist's husband. 'If you see anything, call out for me and hide the others.'

'Yes, Saheb.'

'I might have more work for you later, but first I need to find out what these surgeries will involve.'

'As you say.'

'Do you think, Saheb,' the teacher asked, 'that someone might be suspicious if the clinic lights stay on all night?'

'I sometimes sit here through the night if I can't sleep. The villagers are used to it. But yes, it's possible the light might attract someone. We'll just have to risk that. So, who's first?'

The teacher patted his son's shoulders. 'Operate on him, Saheb, then my wife. Treat me only after you're done with both.'

His wife looked away. From her demeanour, it was clear that this matter had already been decided, that the two had argued over it while the surgeon was away.

The surgeon led the boy to the operating room. The child had appeared quite calm through the evening, but now he hesitated, pulled back at the door. The tiled room seemed to frighten even him, he who had travelled distances that the surgeon couldn't even begin to imagine.

'Go in, my baby,' his mother said. 'It will be done soon. So soon, you won't even realize it.'

The teacher clasped his son's hand. 'I'll be with you. Don't worry.'

The stone slab was covered with a single thin drape, and the surgeon had the boy strip and climb onto it. Over his thin, supine body, his abdomen now rose like a dome, as if he too bore another life within him. His wound still seemed like an elaborate disguise, and the surgeon was tempted to peel back the fake skin and reveal the real one underneath. He hoped that the teacher was right – that the dead couldn't feel any pain. With gloved fingers, he examined the wound and the skin around it, squeezed the sides and pinched the skin, gently at first, and then quite hard between his nails. As promised, the boy felt nothing.

The surgeon adjusted the anglepoise lamps to illuminate the boy's abdomen as best as he could, and with the help of the pharmacist he cleaned the skin and wound with iodine. He then masked and scrubbed and gowned as was customary, swabbed the wound with alcohol, made it sterile, draped it. He took every precaution he would have taken with any other patient. The bodies of the dead might well be immune to infection now, but that would change at dawn. He also took care to arrange the drapes so that the boy wouldn't be able to see his own bowels. Surely there were sights that all humans, alive or dead, were better off not seeing.

With his scalpel in hand, he paused to plan his first incision, and now couldn't help wondering if the dead were just soulless contraptions. Divine puppets, perhaps. Was this a fiendish test, meant to force him to pluck at his core and emerge with god alone knew what? An outrageous test, if so, by a deity who would stoop this low to wring belief from his subjects. What if he were to turn to the stars and cry out, 'I was wrong, I was wrong'? Would the visitors vanish and the three worlds open before him?

He lengthened the wound with his blade, and found himself both fascinated and repulsed by the quality of the boy's flesh. It resembled nothing so much as the flesh of a corpse – not yet mottled or putrid, but dead enough that the blood had coagulated in the vessels and no longer oozed out as he sliced through the skin. It reminded him of his work in the office of the city coroner. Of course, those corpses never climbed up on tables themselves.

The teacher was seated on a low stool next to his son. He whispered and cooed to the boy, ran his fingers through his hair. The boy's eyes were half closed, his hands by his side under the drapes. They remained that way until the surgeon said, 'Maybe this is a good time for you to explain what's going on. Explain how you got here.'

The teacher's eyes, when he raised them, first fell on his son's abdomen, which was in the process of being opened. He immediately jerked them away.

'Are you sure, Saheb?'

'Don't you think I have the right to ask?' replied the surgeon.

'Yes, of course. I didn't mean that. But maybe—maybe you might not want to know.'

'And why would that be?'

'Only the dead know about the afterlife. It's not something the living are supposed to learn.'

'That may be, but all kinds of things are happening tonight that aren't supposed to happen. Besides, if I'm supposed to treat you, I need to understand exactly how the three of you ended up here.'

The teacher looked at his son's face for a few moments, then at the floor.

'The moment we died, all the pain stopped. Then, for who knows how long, we couldn't move. There was no light, no sound, nothing. Slowly, we began to see and hear again. Our senses returned, but not the pain ... thank god, not the pain. We were on this—this plain. It went on and on in all directions. There was no end to it. This was the afterlife, Doctor Saheb, where we all go when we die.

'There were dead people there from every part of the world, all mixed together. They spoke so many different languages, but it was strange, we could understand all of them, and they could understand us. Many had died from old age, others from sickness or epidemics. Some, like us, had been murdered. Our deaths were unjust. Everyone must die some day, yes, but not like this. One person killing another, there's nothing worse than that.

'We met so many people, and each had his own story. Really interesting stories too, from times and places I'd never even heard about. I tried to look for kings or famous people from history but, as you can imagine, most of the dead there were as ordinary as us.'

While the teacher was speaking, the surgeon had deepened the incision in the boy's abdomen through the thin layer of subcutaneous fat. Within the peritoneum, he could see glistening clots in copious volumes. If an injury to a major blood vessel had caused this bleeding, it would be disastrous, impossible to mend here. The question couldn't be answered through the limited aperture of the wound. He would need to make a larger incision, inspect the contents of the entire abdomen through a long vertical cut.

'Weren't you attacked this evening, after sunset? And yet you were on this plain. How much time did you spend there?'

'In the afterlife, there's no way to keep time, Saheb. There's no sun that rises, no days, no weeks. That's not to say it's dark, not at all, but there's just this ... this light that glows. It never becomes any dimmer or brighter. And there's no need for sleep either. When we got there, the shock of everything was so great that we tried to hold on to the one thing that was as natural to our lives as breathing. We tried, we forced ourselves. We would close our eyes, lie down, try to imagine that it was night – even imagine we were dreaming, to see if that would help. In life one sleeps and then dreams – I thought in death maybe it would work the other way around. But that didn't help either. Once you're dead, you don't need any rest, and so we've been awake ever since.

'It's very difficult to describe the way time works there. Here on earth we're always reminded of it – ticking clocks, summer and monsoon, even little things like food on a stove. If you take it off the fire too soon, it's raw, too late and it's burnt – that's a measure of time too. And even if you lock yourself in a room, turn off all the lights, sit in complete silence, you can still hear your heartbeat. There's nothing like that there. Someone mentioned to me in the afterlife that the only point when any living being experiences this kind of time – this absence of time, rather – is inside the womb. But who can claim to have memories of that?

'In any case, to answer your question, Doctor Saheb, after what might have been a week or two, I was completely disoriented. And the opportunity to return here came later, much later. After all that wandering, time is again the most important thing for us tonight. I have to remind myself that it's ticking, that things are different now. Or the same again, depending on how you look at it.'

The surgeon turned to the pharmacist for a pair of forceps. Her masked face was turned away from the surgical field. But she was listening, he could see.

'Then we met a celestial being, you could call him an angel, and we told him about the crime done to us. Not just the crime of being stabbed, Saheb, but the crime of being killed. Not everyone who is stabbed dies. Humans decide whom to stab, but someone up there decides who will live and who won't. It shouldn't have happened. We had never harmed anyone. My son deserved to live and grow and have a family that would care for him when he was old. The angel asked us what we wanted him to do.

'"Send us back," we said. "Let us live again."

'"There are laws even we can't break," the angel told us. "The valley between life and death can only be crossed from one side. Once you're here, it doesn't matter how it happened, how unjust the circumstances. It's done."

'"But then what about rebirth?" we asked. "Our priests insisted it happens. Were they lying?"

'"There is rebirth, yes," the angel replied, 'but not the kind they talk about in your land, where you can be reborn as an insect or a lion, something different each time. You can only be reborn as a human, through a woman's womb. People are chosen for it based on their virtues, based on how they lived their lives. Have faith. You will have the opportunity, but it won't happen right away."'

The surgeon's new incision laid the boy open from the tip of his breastbone to his navel. The surgeon cut through the skin and fat, and then through the fibrous strip running down the midline of the abdomen between the muscles on either side. Once the peritoneum was cut, the solidified blood spread before him like a russet sea. He reached in and started scooping out the clots. This part was more bewildering than anything else so far – the fact that the boy could lie there awake while his bloodstream piled up on a tray next to him. The pile grew larger as the peritoneum emptied out, and the contents of the abdomen became visible.

There was a large cut in the edge of the spleen. It just lay there now, dry and pink and feigning innocence, but one only had to imagine how a puncture that size might have bled in life. It took a good amount of time, but the surgeon scooped out every clump of blood that had collected under the liver, the omentum and in the folds around the intestines. He then carefully searched for other injuries.

When he was done, he placed his instruments on a tray and took a breath.

'Is something wrong, Saheb?'

'Nothing, nothing's wrong. It's just that I've discovered what killed your son.'

The man flinched at this, and the surgeon regretted his choice of words.

'What was it?'

'The knife cut into his spleen.'

'Did it hit anything else?'

'Doesn't seem like it.'

'Does that mean that if—if it had missed the spleen, he might have survived?'

'Yes. Perhaps. Yes.'

The teacher turned away, his lips twisting, his face slowly contorting. He blinked, appeared almost to be in pain himself. Then, shielding his eyes from the surgeon and pharmacist, he buried his face in his son's hair. He cried for the first time that night, at this unexpected moment, as if some barrel of emotion he'd been balancing had just been overturned.

The surgeon coughed – two short, blunt coughs – to master any emotion that threatened to spill from himself at the man's display of anguish. It was a technique he'd perfected early in his training. Perhaps too well, for it'd been far too long since he'd felt any emotion worth mastering. Health itself appeared so bleak a state that sickness and death wrung little pity from him any more. Sometimes, when an invalid's final breaths seemed no more than the last turns of a wheel, leaving behind an object to be removed, charred, turned to ash, and stirred into a riverbed, his indifference terrified even him.

'In a sense, we're lucky it's the spleen,' he said, hoping to clear the gloom. 'If the knife had cut the liver or the intestines, or, god forbid, a big artery, we'd have had no chance at all.'

The teacher raised his head. Not a muscle moved on his face as he listened.

'It won't help if I just stitch the spleen shut. It will bleed again. But I can remove the whole thing – he can live without it. I can't promise you we won't discover new problems in the morning, but this might be all that's needed.'

The man clasped his hands together so hard that his knuckles looked like rows of rounded bones. 'You're our saviour, Doctor Saheb, you're a saint. There's nothing I could possibly do in a thousand years to repay your mercy. Please save my son, Saheb. Please do whatever you think is best.'

He rained kisses on his son's cheeks and forehead. 'Saheb is going to fix you. He's going to make you better.'

The boy, infected with his father's enthusiasm, started to prop himself up on an elbow. 'Shhh,' the teacher said, caressing the boy's brow, trying to calm his son though clearly unable to contain himself. 'Don't move, don't move. Lie down.'

The surgeon let himself be lifted by an unfamiliar, buoyant sensation. The one thing that could have confounded this surgery – the tyranny of a relentless bloodstream – he wouldn't have to face tonight. During the early years of his training, he'd once had to extract the spleen of a young man who was struck by a bus. The spleen, ruptured like an egg, had lain at the bottom of a red pool that constantly refilled itself no matter how much blood he suctioned out. By contrast, this was almost absurdly easy.

'Go on,' he said.

'Yes. Where was I? Yes. The angel. We asked him to just send us back to our old lives, but he refused. So we begged him to let us be reborn, but he told us it wasn't our turn yet, and disappeared. But we called him again.'

'How do you call an angel?'

'You have to think of him, imagine his face, ask for his help, and he appears.'

'Just like that?'

'Not exactly – sometimes it works, sometimes it doesn't. I'm sure angels have their own preferences, whose calls they will answer, whose they won't. For whatever reason, our angel appeared more often to us than any of the other angels did to any of the dead.'

'Why?'

'I really don't know, Saheb. I honestly don't think there was anything special about us, but this angel was definitely different from all the others. In fact, he always had more questions for us than we did for him. He asked us about our families, our childhoods, our wedding, the birth of our son. He was interested in the customs of the living – our festivals and foods, the way we traded money for objects. Even small things – the way we kept our houses, painted our walls, grew potted plants in the yard. He had watched these things from the afterlife, but he didn't always understand what he was seeing.'

'Didn't understand? What do you mean? Wouldn't angels be all-knowing?'

'Well, those are two different things, Saheb: knowing and understanding. I'll give you a simple example. The angel knew that the living like to fly kites, but never understood why it was such a popular thing, why it should deserve a special day of celebration, why people would drop everything and climb on rooftops for it. There are no kites in the afterlife. There's no wind there, not even really a sky ... there's just that plain. I tried to explain to him the joy when something that's nothing more than a square of paper stretched across two sticks catches the breeze and goes up, up ... so high that sometimes you can't even see it against the sun, so high even birds won't get near it. I tried to explain it a few different ways, but none of them made any sense to the angel.

'And so I told him that it felt like toying with death. It

was like tying your life to a thread, sending it out to a place over which you had no power, working all day to keep it from being lost, and then, in the evening, if you were lucky, pulling it back unharmed, admiring its colours again, and storing it in a safe place for another time. That's when the angel understood. That was his language, Doctor Saheb, the language of life and death.'

The teacher's story was like a bizarre fable – something a priest might deliver in a religious ceremony. But there were no flowers here, no lamps or burning incense to make the unreality more palatable. The surgeon felt a constant tightness at the base of his throat. He had to loosen it occasionally by swallowing the spittle in his mouth.

'What do these angels look like?'

'They look human, just like everyone else. No shining eyes, no aura of light. They don't ride on any animals, they don't fly, they walk on their own two feet. Our angel was about my height, shorter than you. He looked a little overweight, but I think their bodies are just disguises they wear in front of us.'

'So what happened next?'

'It became a regular thing. I would call for the angel, and he would appear. I would ask that we be sent back, and he would smile and decline my request. And then he would ask his own questions. I have to admit that even though the likelihood of returning to life seemed to diminish with each of his visits, I still kept calling for him, just to see what new question he would bring me. I've always wanted to help people see things in different ways. That's why I became a teacher. When students couldn't understand something that seemed obvious to me, I took it as a challenge to figure out what the basic misunderstanding was, and use that to explain things better. I don't want to suggest that the angel was my student, of course not. I wouldn't even dare call him a friend. But I valued the time I spent with him, answering his questions.

'And then, during one of his visits, when I wasn't expecting anything at all, he said that there was something he could do for us. Something that was within his power.'

By now the surgeon had freed the spleen of the scaffolding that had held it up against the diaphragm and the other organs. He checked its surfaces and prepared to tie off the vessels that would, in life, have fed it blood. The teacher had paused, so the surgeon looked up at him, signalled that he was still listening.

The teacher glanced at the pharmacist. 'The very first thing the angel said to me was that all of this had to remain secret. I can tell you, Saheb, you have every right to know. But I beg you, none of this can leave the clinic. We were ordered to keep it to the smallest number of people possible. Forget the rest of the world, even the rest of the village cannot know of this.'

The surgeon nodded. He turned to the girl, who nodded as well, though with some hesitation.

'The angel told me that there are limits to what any single one of them can do. Each has a few specific powers. They can perform what we would consider miracles, yes, but only with the skills of four or five put together.

'He offered to send us back, but he didn't have the ability to fix our wounds. He couldn't manipulate human flesh, he said. We would have to return just the way we were. That was enough to dash all my hopes. What were we to do then? Bleed to death again? Empty our lives into the mud? The angel said he could help us in one way – he could keep us from coming alive for some time. He could keep us like this – bloodless, the way we appear to you now – but for no more than one earthly night. That was all. While everyone was asleep, we would have to get our wounds fixed. Blood would start flowing through us at dawn.

'Now, Saheb, you can imagine what I thought when he said this. The offer sounded hopeless enough already, but the restrictions didn't end there. He reminded us again and again that what he was offering was completely forbidden. Apparently, angels can be punished too. By even talking about helping us, he was putting himself at risk. He told us that his power extended only to a small village – this village. He couldn't allow knowledge of this plan to ever spread outside it. No other angel could ever be allowed to see us. We could never cross the boundary. If we tried, our bodies would drop like corpses right there, and we would be pulled back to the afterlife. It also meant that we could never visit our old town; never see our families. We wanted life, didn't we? Well, now we could get it, with all of these conditions binding our hands and feet.

'But I should bite my tongue before I say another ungrateful word. Please understand, I'm not blaming the angel. He was offering us the very best option he had. But still, to be sent here after sunset, with just a night before we died again ... it seemed so pointless. Until he told us that within this village lived a very skilled surgeon.'

The surgeon felt his hands go slack. 'The angel mentioned me? Your angel specifically mentioned me?'

So his paranoia wasn't entirely unjustified, was it? There was a prickle in his hair, a wash of fresh sweat, new rivulets tickling their way down the sides of his neck and face. He pretended to stretch his shoulders, turned his neck this way and that, and looked up at the ceiling so that this sudden wave sweeping over him wouldn't be so obvious.

The plaster of the ceiling was plain grey, featureless except for the metal loop embedded in it. From this angle, and with the shadows cast by the lamps around it, the loop looked like an eye, a single sinister aperture set at the centre of a grey face. He allowed himself to indulge this theatrical cliché. Why not? Why not see eyes everywhere? Even in the bulbs, hot and unblinking? Examining, documenting. Perhaps this really was a test, not of his belief but of his surgical skills. What was the examiner looking for? Would a certificate descend from the clouds to declare him competent? Competent at what?

'Yes, Saheb. That's why he made this offer in the first place. If it weren't for you, he would never even have mentioned it. He told us to consider everything very carefully. We could refuse if we wished, but he would never offer us this choice again. So we accepted.'

It was now time to individually tie off and cut the vessels that streamed, bloodless, from the boy's spleen. The surgeon needed to be meticulous. He couldn't allow the absence of blood to lull him into complacency. A single untied vessel, and that would be the end – an open tap through which the boy's life would gush out in the morning. The phalanxes of questions within him would have to wait.

The surgeon ligated the vessels, freed the spleen, and then scooped out the fleshy organ and placed it on a tray. The boy craned his neck forward while this was happening, but his father patted him back, covered his eyes. The surgeon inspected the liver, the stomach, the intestines, the vessels again. Once he was as certain as he could possibly be that the murderer's blade had missed them all, he picked a long, thin strip of corrugated rubber from his tray. He threaded it in through the stab wound, and positioned the inner end within the peritoneal bed where the spleen had been. The other end he kept free against the skin on the outside. It would catch and drain any blood that might leak through the vessels and pool in the abdomen in the morning, he explained.

Then he sutured back the layers of flesh, one after the other. Once the skin was closed and dressed, he tried to make the scene less grisly by covering the spleen and the pile of clots with a drape. The boy had said nothing during the surgery, but now he looked impatient, eager to be done.

'Careful, don't sit up too quickly. The stitches are delicate. You don't feel them now, but you could pull them out if you run around too much. And don't touch the bandages. They need to remain clean.'

The boy listened with just half his attention, but his father nodded at everything.

The surgeon began to list to the girl the instruments he wanted sterilized right away, but stopped when he actually looked at her. She hadn't spoken during the surgery, and the parts of her face visible between the green stripes of her mask and cap were as bleached as the moon.

Seven

Out in the corridor, the teacher's wife clutched her son and covered him with kisses. For the first time that night, their despair seemed to have lifted. The surgeon looked away, wondering if, in his optimism, he had promised too much. Their expectations would be even greater now. And the boy might succumb to any number of complications in the morning.

Supporting the pharmacist, the surgeon stepped into the night. Gravel crunched under his feet.

The girl's husband ran up to them and put his arm around her, saying, 'It's all right, it's all right.' He caressed her hair, pressed her into his neck. She leaned against him, pale and stiff.

He cast a fearful glance at the dead. 'Did they do anything to her?'

The surgeon compressed his lips and winced, afraid that the family had overheard this needless slander. 'Just sit her down somewhere. She's not used to this. Nothing more.'

The man led his wife to a flat rock a few yards away. She sat there with her arms wrapped around her ribs.

During her time in the clinic, the pharmacist had assisted in childbirths and minor procedures, learnt how to change dressings, clean ulcers, administer injections. But she'd never taken part in a surgery in which the depths of the bowels were plumbed and the organs carved out. With his mind so crowded with otherworldly matters, the surgeon had overlooked this simple fact. Perhaps it was best he kept her out of the operating room from this point on.

Apart from the whispering of the dead in the corridor, the silence was almost deliberate – as if the crickets had been bribed and the dogs strangled. The village at the base of the hillock was perfectly still, its houses like polyps erupting from the soil. The rising moon had dusted them all with white talc. They appeared to have receded in the hours after sunset, abandoning the clinic to its unnatural deeds.

The surgeon returned to his consultation room. From a drawer in his desk, he picked out a syringe, a needle and two thumb-sized glass vials with rubber corks. From a jar of anticoagulant salt from a shelf, he tapped a few crystals into each vial. In another drawer, he found small paper labels. He wrote a couple of words on two and pasted them around the sides of the vials. With his left sleeve rolled up all the way to his shoulder, he tied a tourniquet around his biceps, pulling the end of the loop with his teeth until blue veins bulged on his forearm. Then he guided the needle into one of them, drew the plunger back with a thumbnail, and pulled out half a syringe of blood. This he divided between the vials, tilting and turning them until the crystals dissolved. Some empty thermocol boxes had been left over from the vaccination drive. He filled one of them with ice cubes from the refrigerator.

He then began drafting his list. He would only have one opportunity. This wasn't the time to rush, to forget something important. He wrote and erased, crossed things out, calculated, estimated. Would eight of this item be better than four? Would twenty of those suffice? Maybe the larger ones instead of the smaller? There were limits to what he could ask for, of course. He had to be realistic.

When he was satisfied – or rather, when he was done – he waved to the pharmacist's husband. The man was with his wife. It took the surgeon a couple of attempts to catch his eye.

If indeed this entire fantastic premise was true, and the sun would melt the clotted blood in the vessels of these visitors, the challenges of this night would pale before those that the dawn would bring. Since all medical care would have to take place within the walls of this clinic, the pharmacist's husband would need to travel to the city for supplies. He would have to fetch intravenous lines, tubing, catheters, sutures, needles, syringes, gauze, bandages, antibiotics, tetanus vaccine, lidocaine, opiates, sedatives. The clinic would have to be stocked as never before. There were some bags of saline in the pharmacy and, while those would likely not be enough, it was unreasonable to expect the man to bring back more than a few litres. If those ran out too, they would have to make do with boiled, salted tap water and accept the risks.

But perhaps the most important of these requirements was blood. Who could predict which stitches would hold and which would give way, and what streams would flow unstemmed?

The surgeon placed the blood-filled vials in a small box and handed them to the man. 'List me as the patient in the blood bank. Get four bags. Bring more if they'll allow you. Make sure they cross-match it well. It needs to match my blood type exactly. O-negative. Look, I've written it right here. If you get the correct match, it should be safe to transfuse into anyone.'

From his safe, he picked out a small bundle held together by a rubber band, and counted the notes before handing them over.

'This should be enough for everything, I hope.'

The man's eyes kept flitting to the window.

'Perhaps I should first ask you,' the surgeon said, 'if you would be willing to let her stay here while you're gone.'

The man shifted his weight from one foot to the other without answering.

'They won't harm her.' The surgeon hoped his tone was reassuring. 'That much I can say.'

The man fidgeted and scratched his ear, turned the list over a few times. Then he nodded with the resignation of one unaccustomed to challenging instructions. 'I should leave now, if I'm to get back before morning.'

He went to the back room and picked out a bedsheet from the cupboard. Then he slipped out quietly through the corridor, careful to keep as great a distance as possible between himself and the dead, to the point that the surgeon saw him almost jump into a wall when the teacher tried to thank him. There was an old pile of bamboo rods outside the clinic. The man picked a thin one, waved it around to make sure it was sturdy, and fashioned a makeshift sling with the bedsheet. He then walked his bicycle to the pharmacist, spoke to her briefly and pedalled off. The surgeon watched him through the bars of his window. The railway station was a few miles away. Even if the stars all lined up, it would be at least two hours by train to the city.

The surgeon walked to the rock. The pharmacist hadn't moved from her spot since her husband had brought her there.

'You look tired. It's very late.'

She sat looking out into the darkness. The surgeon flicked a mosquito from his neck.

'You won't have to be in the operating room with me any more. I can see that it's too much for you.'

The rattle of the bicycle had completely faded by now.

'But it would be good if I could still have your help. I've already used half of the instruments and drapes, and there are two more surgeries left. While I operate on the woman, could you wash and autoclave the used items? You don't have to stay awake all night – in fact I don't want you to. You could turn the drum on and then take a nap in the back room. I'll wake you when I'm done.'

She said nothing. The surgeon sat beside her on the rock, his joints making their usual clicking sounds.

'Maybe I should do a fourth surgery tonight. After I'm done with the dead, I should just replace my knees with oiled hinges.'

There was a feeble smile at this.

He was asking too much of her, he knew. It wasn't fair to expect her to brush aside all her fear and disorientation for his sake, just because he'd taken upon himself this delusion of reviving the dead. It would be better if she went home.

But before he could suggest it, she asked, 'Could this be a mistake, Saheb?'

'Mistake?'

'The man says that the angel doesn't want him to leave this village. Isn't that something to worry about?'

'Yes, it is. It's very worrying. Even if your husband returns with every single item on that list, it still won't be anywhere near to what's necessary for something like this. But what can we do? We work with what we have.'

'Forgive me, Saheb, but that wasn't what I meant. I was talking about ... about this being a secret. That's what I'm worried about.'

'What do you mean?'

'They're breaking the law. The dead man didn't say it that way, but he knows what he's doing. He knows it's not allowed, coming back like this, like corpses. And now he wants *us* to break the law too. What if some evil spirit sent them here against God's wishes? What if it's a sin to help them? I'm afraid, Saheb. I am nobody to question you, but what will happen to us? Won't we be punished with them?'

The surgeon looked up at the sky. It seemed charred, as if some great and distant immolation had finally been completed. When he was the girl's age, already filled with doubt about everything he'd ever been told, he'd wondered how astrologers assembled all those creatures from the stars – rams and fishes and scorpions. All he ever saw were silent threats – the way the dots of light hung there, deceptively stable from one night to the next, preparing to dash themselves to the earth at the slightest provocation.

'Ask any priest and he will tell you exactly what God wants you to do. What prayer, what fasts, what lockets and threads to wear. And then ask another, maybe an imam or father this time, and see what answer you get. There are many people who pretend to know God's wishes. But God Himself never says a word.'

'But then, Saheb, how do we know what to do? How do we know we're not doing something wrong tonight?'

'We cannot know,' said the surgeon, surprised at the bitterness in his own voice. 'We cannot know. That's the most difficult thing about this, and not just tonight. We hope that before we die we'll find some final truth, a magic bulb to switch on and make all the wrong paths disappear. Until then, all we can do is walk through thorns and try not to trip.'

'Then why not leave it to fate, Saheb? Whatever will happen, let it happen. Why try to change it?'

There was an ache in his calf. He was tempted to remain seated on the rock and indulge it; rest while he ruminated on the questions the girl kept tossing at him. But she was too young. Maybe she thought her doubts original, and maybe someday he would have time enough to explain to her just how ancient they were, and how unanswerable.

But now it was almost eleven. He raised himself with his palms anchored on his thighs, straightening his knees first and then his spine. He was an old man now. His reluctant bones had to be prodded into motion.

They were at the very edge of a circle that the clinic lights had carved from the darkness. Beyond it, a cloud blotted out the moon. A few selfish fireflies idled in the grass, doing nothing to illuminate the shape moving up the hillock. It wasn't an animal, that was all the surgeon could tell. And it wasn't on a bicycle.

He pressed a finger to his lips. 'Shhh...'

The pharmacist raised her head, confused, and then she too saw. For a moment she sat there, as frozen as he. Then she said, 'I'll hide them,' and headed to the clinic.

Eight

No, it was too absurd. That he could even think it was evidence enough of his slipping mind. Why would an angel appear in this way? He could materialize from the air, spy on them through walls. He wouldn't trudge up with this slow, ominous walk.

But then why was he himself clinging to his little limbus of light? If it was some villager – and who else could it possibly be? – surely it'd be better to stop him as far from the clinic as possible. And if it were indeed the angel, what shield would the dim light provide? Yet, the surgeon found himself unable to step forward. It wasn't fear, he insisted. And what if it were? The hour was late, after all. Why not remain where he had a sliver of an advantage against some madman with a knife?

Hushed words were uttered behind him. A door closed, soft and slow as the creak of a tree. The angle from which the visitor was approaching wouldn't allow him to see directly into the clinic. For that at least, the surgeon was thankful.

'Doctor Saheb.'

The voice was slurred, and the surgeon instantly recognized it. A mortal, and the basest of them all. His blood rose into his temples.

'What are you doing here? This late?'

The man was closer now, his rosaceous nose entering the light before the rest of him did. He was taking one step at a time, as if confirming that the first knee wouldn't betray him before he trusted the next with his weight.

'My leg, Doctor Saheb.'

'What happened to your leg?'

'Blood, so much blood.'

The man's dhotar was folded to the middle of his thighs, and his shins were coated with mud. He had the breeze at his back, and even at this distance, the surgeon could smell the stench. Alcohol and vomit, and everything else about him.

'What blood? I don't see anything?'

'Look, Saheb.'

'Stand right there. Don't come any closer.'

The surgeon twisted his neck back. The corridor was empty. The girl had managed to conceal them in time. The man walked past him, made for the clinic. The surgeon considered reaching out and grabbing him, but the very thought of touching the drunkard made his nerves curl.

'Go home. It's late, I don't have time for you now.'

The man started wailing at a grating pitch. 'Doctor Saheb, the blood, do something. I'm dying.'

'Quiet. What nonsense is this? It's just a little scratch. Go home.'

'I won't go back. Why should I return to her? She threw me out, at this time, this late, Doctor Saheb. What kind of wife—'

On any other night, all the surgeon would have had to do was cup his mouth and yell in the direction of the village, and a few strong farmers would come and muscle the man away. But now the dog was already at the clinic entrance.

'What do you want? Money? Here, take this and go.'

The man studied the two notes the surgeon had pulled from his wallet, grasped at them. His hand missed a few times, and then he let a wave of martyrdom wash over him.

'Don't want it, Doctor Saheb. What'll I do with money? Money is for educated people like you. Not for us. We'll stay this way, live and die in the ditch.'

The man was actually bleeding, the surgeon could now see. There was a cut on his calf.

'Sit right here, on the grass. I'll bandage you up. Do you promise you'll leave after that?'

'Yes, Saheb, I'll go, I swear on my mother's ashes, my father's ashes. They're both dead. I swear on them, I'll go.' With these words, the man lurched into the corridor.

The surgeon scrambled ahead, squeezed past the drunkard. The doors to the pharmacy, the back room and the operating room were all closed – hopefully bolted from the inside so that if the man fell into them, they wouldn't fly open. Only the door of the consultation room was ajar. The surgeon confirmed with a quick look that no one was hiding there.

The man collapsed on a bench. The surgeon had to bite back the urge to kick him out, physically toss him on the gravel. Who cared if he broke a bone or two? How could the dead, with their corpse-like bodies, smell less revolting than this living creature?

Under the lights, the gash in the man's calf was more visible. The surgeon considered just bandaging it and sending the man away, but that wouldn't work. The bandage would soak through, and then he'd be back.

'You'll need a few stitches. Don't move. Do you understand?'

'Yes, Saheb.' There were red cobwebs around the man's irises.

All the supplies were in the operating room. The surgeon walked up to the door and pushed the handle, but it was latched from the inside.

'I'll check here,' he said in a raised voice, as if to no one in particular, and tapped his knuckle softly on the doorframe.

The latch on the inside clicked. He looked back at the bench. The man was still there, his leg stretched in front of him, the rest of his body bent sideways like a sack of grain. He didn't seem to have noticed. The surgeon stepped in and latched the door shut behind him.

The pharmacist was there, sweat beading her brow along the line of her hair. 'Where are they?' he mouthed, and she pointed towards the back room.

The lamps were all switched off, and only the ghost of the moon seeped in through the thick, frosted windows.

In the near dark, he put on a pair of gloves and picked out a needle and thread, some cotton and gauze and tape, a bottle of iodine, a small tray. He also picked up his very last vial of lidocaine. Not out of compassion, it had to be said. He just couldn't afford to have a screaming man in his clinic now. The trays around the operating table were as he'd left them – the instruments, the spleen, the clots, all there under a blood-drenched drape. Drained of colour by the moon, the drape glistened in silvers and greys. It was terrible to leave the pharmacist in the dark in a room like this, but what else could he do?

She didn't need to be told. She flattened herself against the wall as he opened the door.

The drunkard had wandered from his bench. He was at the door of the back room, trying to rattle it open.

'What are you doing? I told you to sit there, didn't I?' He grabbed the man's shoulder, pushed him down the corridor, forced him back where he was.

The man was blabbering. 'I was trying to find you, Saheb. Didn't know where you went.'

The surgeon knelt down and placed his tray on the floor. He'd forgotten the forceps. With his gloved fingers, he bundled a piece of cotton, soaked it with iodine and swabbed the wound. He then drew the lidocaine into the syringe.

'This may burn a little.' He guided the needle into the edge of the wound.

'Oh god,' the man cried out when he was pierced. 'Save me, it hurts so much, I'm dying, I'm dying.'

The surgeon ground his jaw. He'd seldom felt such rage. The man yelled as the surgeon stuck the needle in at one angle and then another, into the right edge of the wound and then the left, emptying the lidocaine into the wound. Then the surgeon raised his face to the drunkard and roared, 'Shut up or I'll smash your teeth in.'

The man cowered under him, muttered something incoherent. A black crust coated his gums – the foul residue of tobacco he'd been chewing on for god knew how long. The surgeon felt the urge to retch.

But the lidocaine worked. The man didn't even notice when the suturing started. It was a pity there was no drug to paralyse his tongue.

'She's a whore. She lets anyone enter her. Nothing but a whore. I should charge the neighbours – fifty rupees to look, another fifty to touch between her thighs, another fifty to spread them and—'

'Don't you have any shame, talking about your wife this way? You could search for ten lifetimes and never find someone like her. You beat her every night, and still she stays with you, I have no idea why. Any other woman would have returned to her parents by now.'

'Her parents are dead too. All gone. Ashes, Doctor Saheb, it's what everyone becomes in the end. No difference between a man and the wood they use to burn him. And I'm telling you, I never touched a bottle before my marriage. Ask anyone, ask the sarpanch if you want. All of this, it was only after she—she came to my house, the *witch*. *She* did this to me, turned me into this.'

The surgeon tried to block him out.

'Don't want this life, nothing of it. Better to be dead than to live like this.'

'Stop talking and let me do my work.'

'I'm telling you, Saheb, I have a bottle of rat poison. After I go back tonight, I'm going to drink it, drink the whole bottle. Don't want this life.'

The man had done this thrice already, his theatrical attempts at suicide. He'd swallowed some DDT the last time, then walked to the village square to beat his chest and announce it to one and all. They'd brought him to the clinic with his beard white with powder, more DDT outside his mouth than inside it. But the surgeon did what he had to do. He put a tube down the man's nose, washed out the contents of his stomach, pumped it full of charcoal powder to absorb any remaining poison. The man then vomited all over the clinic, and the smell took forever to wash out of the mattresses. The same farce now, on this of all possible nights. This imbecile threatening to take his pathetic life while the dead waited in the next room for a resurrection. And it was half past eleven already.

'If you want to kill yourself, why are you here at all? Why do you want me to stitch up this scratch? Just go home and drink your poison. And lock yourself in your room so that no one brings you here half-alive again. I hope that when they find you, your bones are as cold as ice, and you're gone, once and for all.'

These words penetrated even the drunkard's thick, intoxicated skull. His eyes opened wide and he slumped back, finally silent.

The surgeon finished stitching the wound and knotted the ends of the sutures together. Not a drop of blood squeezed through them. He rolled a bandage around the calf and shin and taped it in place.

'Up.' He lifted the man without taking off his gloves, steered him out.

The drunkard pushed up against the wall, tried to slither out of his grip. 'I know who you're hiding.'

Had the man seen? 'What are you talking about?'

'What will the villagers think, Saheb? It's not right.'

'Just say what you have to say or get out.'

'Does it suit you, someone of your position? With that girl? I saw her run in and hide. Look at your age, look at hers. And she's married too.'

The surgeon felt fury burn his throat. 'Go. And if you ever come back, I swear I'll smash every single bone in your body.'

The drunkard showed real fear now. Perhaps the alcohol was wearing off. He almost lost his footing on the two short steps and limped his way down the hillock, turning back once or twice but not stopping. The surgeon stood at the clinic entrance, arms crossed, as though he were the keeper of some forbidden cave.

'He's gone. You can come out now.'

The dead emerged in a huddle from the back room. The boy clutched at his mother, shrinking behind her when the surgeon looked at him. The surgeon couldn't help his irritation at this. What did they expect him to do, keep up some charade of benevolence all night? There were limits.

He wasn't a saffron-clad monk. If they couldn't put up with the way he did things, they were free to leave.

Yes, he remembered now, he'd been talking to the pharmacist when the bastard interrupted them. She hadn't appeared from the operating room.

He pushed the door open. She was clearing away the trays. She'd already gathered the soiled drapes, and was emptying some of the remains into a plastic bag.

'You should go home and sleep,' he said with a dismissive wave.

'No, Saheb. You working through the night alone? What will my husband say when he returns? I'll sterilize the instruments.'

Nine

Whatever triumph the surgeon had let himself feel after mending the boy's injury was completely dulled now, partly by his lingering ire over the drunkard, more at the prospect of facing the woman's wounds. He felt a deep resentment against all creation for putting him in this position. Why had the neck been designed this way in the first place? All those vessels, so close to the skin. Countless necks had been slit since man sharpened his first stone, but each new one came into existence as flimsy as the last.

The woman's odhni hid her injuries, and the three appeared deceptively whole, a family like any other. Apart from the pallor of their skin, there was no hint of their trials and migrations, or of the strangeness of their bodies. When he said, 'Come,' the woman patted down her hair and adjusted her clothes. Even in death, it seemed, the habits of life were not entirely lost.

'The two of you should stay here,' he said to the teacher and his son.

The woman tried to pull her fingers from her son's grip, but the boy kept grabbing at them, higher and higher, tugging at her hand, her wrist, her forearm, first one side, then the other. The teacher tried to restrain him, and the boy resisted, but neither made a sound. Father and son grappled in pantomime until they were locked, larger fists imprisoning smaller ones as though doubled in prayer.

The pharmacist wasn't done clearing the operating room, so the surgeon walked to the entrance and surveyed the hillock for loiterers. Nothing he could do would jeopardize the woman's life beyond what was already fated, he told himself. It was tempting to adopt the pharmacist's way of thinking about the world and everything in it. Whatever would happen would happen, she'd said ... or something similar, some aphorism of endless absolving circularity.

Without turning, he said to the dead: 'This will take at least a few hours. You'll have to be patient.' He cast one last look outside. There was no sign of the drunkard, or the pharmacist's husband, or anyone else.

In the operating room, he now became aware of another astonishing aspect of the visitors' physiology, if that word could even be applied to the bodily mechanisms of the dead. Before the first surgery, he'd listened to the boy's chest with his stethoscope, more out of custom than with any specific intention, for what changes would he have made to his plan had his findings been abnormal? And abnormal they certainly were. The boy had no heartbeat, which, given that there was no blood to flow, wasn't particularly unexpected. It would've been more startling if the familiar *lub dub, lub dub* had reached his ears. But the boy breathed, and his chest rose and fell. The stethoscope confirmed the steady tide blowing through the maze of his airways. Now what need could there be for respiration when there was no blood to be oxygenated? No obvious answer presented itself, and since the boy's injuries involved only his abdomen, the surgeon abandoned that line of questioning and proceeded with the surgery.

But in the case of the woman, due to the nature and location of her injuries, he was forced to give the mechanics of her breathing greater attention. Her larynx was cut in such a way that there was a good chance her vocal cords had been damaged. And the cut had definitely produced an air leak, a direct connection between the inside and outside of her throat. How could she possibly speak with such an injury?

This led him to an extraordinary discovery – a phenomenon every bit as bizarre as her silent heart. Her voice appeared to form not in her larynx but in the back of her mouth, somewhere in the space behind her tonsils – from empty air as best as he could tell. How that could possibly be, he hadn't a clue. Her speech was unconnected to her lungs and her voice box, and though her words were coordinated with her breathing, they didn't seem to depend on it in any way. He found that she could, with little effort, overcome the innate habits of her body and speak without interruption throughout both inhalation and exhalation. And, astonishingly, even with her breath held.

The anatomy of the dead was incomprehensible. Some of their bodily systems worked, others didn't, but it was all just enough to allow them to impersonate the living. If his old EKG machine hadn't been roasted by a power surge, he would've taken tracings from their chests. What scrawls might the box have produced? Waves and peaks? Flat, monotonous lines? Or something else? Patterns, letters, perhaps; messages in some ancient, unbreakable code. Equations containing the deepest enigmas of death. He would keep the tracings running endlessly, paper every wall with EKG strips. Years, perhaps decades later, when his mind had become weak and every memory doubtful, he could return to read the chronicle of these hours plastered from floor to ceiling. Perhaps then he would see everything more clearly.

The disconnect between the woman's voice and her larynx resolved a purely practical concern. He'd expected that the surgery would leave her unable to speak. He'd been in half a mind to tell her that – to have her say to her husband and son whatever she needed to say while she still could. But this fear no longer appeared warranted. No matter what he did, she would still be able to speak. At least until dawn.

But this insight could not blunt the savagery he was seeing. The surgeon gritted his teeth, pressed his lips together, forced his face to remain expressionless as he examined her. The tips of her earlobes were torn; the sides of her arms scraped raw, skin peeled away along the bony parts of her wrists. The bandits had been thorough in their plunder, ripped out her earrings, torn off her bangles. But the wound in her neck ... The hand that did this had not sought only money. There was craving here, a hunger for whatever arousal was to be gained by sinking a blade into flesh. This was no theft complicated by unintended murder.

Before this night, he'd found it easy to fill medical silences with chiding banter and rebuke, but none of that could help him now. No words of consolation, nothing he could dredge up, held any truth or meaning. All speech was blasphemy before these wounds. And then there was her massive abdomen, looming at the edge of his vision. He couldn't speak of that either. Surely it was never far from her mind, but what purpose would it serve to bring it up, to remind her that the life of another creature hung in the balance of her own?

Decades ago, when he was working at the coroner's office, he'd been assigned the autopsy of a young woman who'd hanged herself after learning that her husband had frequented a brothel during her pregnancy. She would have been at term in a few weeks, and in her suicide note, she wrote of her intention to free herself of this unjust life and take her child with her. And that she did, for on the slab, her thin corpse was distended with what lay still within her. As part of regular autopsy protocol, he was required to extract the inhabitant of her womb, a cold and unmoving foetus that had never known the world outside her and now never would.

Later that day, unexpected visitors had knocked on his office door.

'Doctor Saheb.'

Raising his eyes from his papers, he, a young man then, saw two aged, myopic faces.

'The girl on whom you performed an autopsy today ... we're her parents.'

'The morgue is to the left. A man there will have you sign some paperwork, and then you can take her for your rites. It shouldn't take much time.'

It was a perfunctory response, his attempt to make the meaninglessness of death bearable through protocol. If only mourners could just occupy themselves with the mechanics of planning a funeral. Second door to the left. Sign here, here and here, that form too. And don't forget to write the address of the crematorium.

But this elderly couple couldn't be dismissed so easily. They stood there, waiting for something else.

He peeled his glasses off his head and laid them on the desk. It was a trite gesture, but it helped him offer his trite sympathies. 'It's so terrible this happened. So terrible you have to bear this. My condolences.'

'Did she really take her own life?' the mother asked.

His throat felt dry. He now noticed two shabby, discoloured bags on the floor behind them. They'd just travelled here from some distant village. Probably on the first bus they could board, jostled for hours by strangers who had no idea how their world had just been smashed. There was a good chance this morgue, and maybe his office, was their first destination from the railway station. Perhaps all they knew of her death was the little they'd been told over a bad telephone connection.

'Did she really take her own life?' she asked again.

What answer was he supposed to give? The simplest and truest?

'Yes, she did.'

From beyond the swinging door came a distant guffaw. The attendants in the common room were sharing some lunchtime joke.

'But why?' the mother cried. 'Why didn't she just come to us? Did she think we wouldn't take her back?'

All he could do was fidget with the pen in his hand.

And then she asked, 'Was it a boy or a girl?'

Her words fell on his ears but did not sink in.

'Was it a boy or a girl?' she asked once more.

'A boy or a girl?' he repeated. Then the meaning of her question dawned on him. 'Why are you asking me that? Why do you want to know?'

The woman put her palms together. 'Forgive me, Doctor Saheb. We know you're busy. We won't take any more of your time. Please tell us if it was a boy or a girl, and we'll go.'

'It was a boy,' he said, faltering, and then corrected himself. 'It would have been a boy.'

At this, the old woman clasped her bony fists to her mouth and sobbed, as though with his words he had made flesh before her the tiny hands and toes and lips of her unseen grandchild. And not just that, but also the swollen face of her daughter and the furrow of that noose imprinted in her neck. He closed his eyes and turned away. The swinging door creaked as it swung again, and even after it stopped, he could still hear the sobs as the old man led his wife away.

In the coroner's office, he steeled his heart against his work, dissociated from the subjects that lay uncomplaining on his slab. After all, what hope would he have of keeping his sanity if he took it upon himself to probe into the life of every corpse? He only needed to think of them as clocks that had stopped, and of himself as the watchmaker assigned to list the springs and coils that had failed. No obligation to repair anything. He did this for two years, but then it became too oppressive, and he wanted something more. The empty ambition of youth, as he thought of it now. Look what it had brought him.

'I'll have to shave your hair,' he said to the teacher's wife.

She looked startled. 'All of it?'

'Just the back of your neck and a little way up. Is that all right?'

'Yes, Saheb, I didn't mean to question you. Whatever you need to do.'

'Put on this gown.'

He thought of stepping out of the room so that she could change in private, but it would require him to reshuffle the cart and trays he had arranged in the cramped space behind him. So he just cleared his throat and turned to the wall. Behind his back, the dead woman undressed from the waist up and slipped on the tattered green surgical gown.

'I'm ready.'

Using a fresh razor, he shaved her nape and the back of her head. Fine strands fell on her shoulders. The hair of the dead, no more or less dead than the hair of the living. He brushed it into a tray. The rest of her hair he helped bundle into a surgical cap. He positioned her, neck arched backward, head elevated with wooden blocks, contorted into a pose that would allow him full advantage of the meagre light. The position would have been unbearable to anyone capable of feeling pain, but he found that she could hold it without complaint, as if she were a mannequin. After cleaning her wounds with iodine and alcohol, he draped her so that only her neck and its injuries were exposed. Only when he'd laid a drape across her face, covering her eyes, did his shoulders relax a fraction. He didn't want her looking at him while he worked. He could not bear her unreasonable hope.

Her neck had suffered at least two deep strokes and a few shallower ones. The skin was shredded and hung in strips, and the tissues beneath were sliced at jagged angles. Some muscles had been partially cut as well, even the one that was supposed to be necessary for her to turn her head. That she could support and move it naturally despite this was as remarkable as her ability to speak.

Part of the larynx lay open before him in a macabre display of cartilage. Now, with her neck bent back, air puffed through the opening with every breath. Blood vessels with dull red clots within them poked out of the ravaged mess. The most prominent vessel – the carotid artery – was also the one that had suffered the most ominous damage, for the two deepest knife strokes had cut into it at different angles, detaching a flap from one of its sides. This had carved a window into the vessel, through which her blood had probably spurted out with such speed that her suffering had likely been the shortest of the three. But the flap had somehow stayed in place, attached by a strip of tissue so narrow that he was surprised it hadn't fallen off in the few hours since she'd appeared in his clinic. If it had, there would have been a gaping hole in the vessel, and nothing here would have allowed him to close that.

He wasn't trained to deal with injuries like these, to the neck, to the larynx. Even recalling some of the fascial planes, the names of the smaller muscles, the positions of the nerves, was beyond him now. There was a volume of anatomy in his cupboard somewhere, three decades old at least, its binding tattered. He wished he'd thought to skim through it earlier, but it was too late for that now, and he wasn't sure it would have helped. He would have to feign a mastery he did not possess, and braid together the frayed threads of her life as best he could.

He unwrapped the suture casing and grasped with his forceps his thinnest needle and suture. With it he pierced the lower half of the carotid stub. The needle made too large a hole in the gossamer structure, and the suture looked thick and unwieldy, a jute rope hooped through silk. He passed the needle through the corresponding point in the upper half of the vessel and tried to bring the two edges together, but one of the ends had retracted between the muscles of the neck, and his thread tugged at the vessel's edge, threatening to tear it. Only the first stitch, and already there were premonitions of defeat. In slow, painstaking loops, his needle crept one stitch at a time around the curve of the vessel.

The night wore on, his back stiffening as he stooped over his work. Finally, with difficulty, he stood upright again. Over an hour had likely passed since the surgery began, and the woman hadn't made a sound, hadn't moved, hadn't so much as inflated her chest. Surely she was just holding her breath to help him, but perhaps it wasn't a bad idea to confirm that she was still there, still alive. Though *alive* wasn't the right word, of course. There was no vocabulary for this kind of thing.

'Is everything fine?' he asked.

There was a movement under the covers, lips brushing against drapes, neck muscles twitching as she moved her jaw to speak. Was that even necessary, though? Maybe the dead could speak like ventriloquists if they wished, with mouths slack and tongues still.

'Yes, Saheb.'

'Any pain? Any discomfort? Do you need to change your position?'

'No, Saheb, don't worry about me.'

It was remarkable how one could get accustomed to even such things. The surgeon no longer felt the deep, acrid bite of moments like these. He could speak calmly to a woman whose neck lay open before him, forceps sticking out between her cartilage and muscles. A glaze of unreality had settled over everything, as though his vision had permanently warped.

He looked up at the wall to his right, but it was bare. He'd forgotten to hang the clock up again after he changed its battery. And he'd removed his wristwatch and left it on his desk in the other room. Unless he either broke his sterile field and ventured out of the room, or called out to the pharmacist, who was probably sleeping as he'd instructed her to, he had no way of knowing what time it was. He closed his eyes for a moment, trying to add up every stitch he'd placed and multiply that number by the time each one had taken, and at once devious sleep hooked its anchors on his eyelids. He opened them in panic and stamped hard on one foot with the other, making his toe pulse with pain. It was still night. He had to stay awake.

Pushing all other thoughts away, he again took stock of the surgical field. All of this time spent, and so little accomplished. He'd sutured the upper edge of the carotid flap to the margin from which it had been torn, and just begun working on the other. The flap bristled with sutures. Clumsier than the precise work he'd once been capable of, his stitching had pulled and constricted the artery into an angular shape, as though an unskilled plumber had forced together a series of crooked and ill-fitting pipes. And the hole in the vessel still gaped. Any attempt to close it would only twist it further.

The fluorescent light emitted a low electric buzz that he hadn't noticed before. Outside the window, a lone crow cawed – a cry of insomnia and longing, if indeed the fauna of this earth were subject to the same torments as mankind. He looked up at the metal loop in the ceiling and shifted his neck this way and that, but it no longer seemed like an eye. It just returned to him the bland look of an inanimate object. The ceiling had no sight, nor did anything beyond it. The dead had been flung at his feet and abandoned.

What was he going to say to them? How would he tell them that she wouldn't survive?

The sweat was making his brow itch, and he dabbed at it with his sleeve, careful not to let his glove touch anything that might not be sterile. He abandoned the suturing of the carotid artery for now. He would tackle the trachea instead.

'This part of your throat, the part through which air flows to your lungs, it's damaged. If I leave it this way, you'll have trouble breathing in the morning. So I'll have to make another hole right here, lower in your neck. To help the air flow.'

The surgeon explained the plan with as much optimism as he could summon up, and the woman nodded under the drapes. Whether she understood a word, he had no way of knowing. She would have nodded at anything he said.

He rolled his gloved fingers over the skin that covered the cartilaginous bumps under her larynx, and decided on an appropriate spot at the midline of the neck, just a little above the point where the collarbones met the sternum. It would have to be a little lower than was customary, yes. The murderer hadn't thought of surgical convenience when he slashed with his blade. The surgeon sliced the skin cleanly and teased away the thin, bloodless layers of tissue with his knife and forceps, pushing aside the muscles that ran like straps along either side of the trachea. Her thyroid was a little larger than he'd expected, and its bridge gripped and covered the front of the trachea. He cut through it. Now he could feel the tracheal rings, and he made a neat cut through them as well. Even though he had no need to fear that she would die on him, his heart still pounded at this step from force of ancient habit. He didn't have a tracheostomy tube, but he'd managed to dig out an endotracheal tube from some old supplies. He inserted one end into the trachea and closed the skin around it. The other end protruded from the neck, and he harnessed it to the skin with loop after loop of suture. The sutures slipped against the smooth plastic, and some fell loose even as he placed them. The tube wasn't designed to be tied like this. He secured it as best he could.

Then he turned to the larynx and began to sew the torn sections of cartilage back together. It was slow, painstaking work, and there was really no way to hurry. There were other arteries and veins too. Diligently he addressed them, trying to pretend that the most crucial problems had been resolved, and now he was just finessing the details. But the carotid would determine whether she lived or died, there was no doubt about that. He felt like a labourer pressing a thousand pellets of clay into hairline cracks in a breached dam, as if all of that toil would somehow compensate for the enormous rift in the centre. Holding sleep at bay with every blink, he focused on the blood vessels, one by one, reconnecting some, tying the superfluous ones into blind stumps.

Finally there was nothing left to do but put the last sutures in the flap of the carotid. As he tightened the last knot, he couldn't help but cringe. But he could either do this or just leave it open, and there was no possible world in which the second choice was the better of the two. The result was terribly unsatisfactory. The vessel looked deformed. There was none of the craftsmanship of which he'd once thought himself capable. He imagined the vessel pulsing with blood, and then imagined it immediately tearing or clotting.

He stitched the torn ends of the muscles together and closed the tissue planes. There was no clean incision along which to close the skin, so he sewed it back along the lines of its rupture, along the blueprint that the murderer had forced upon him. The jagged rows of stitches looked like railway tracks placed by a deranged engineer, crossing each other at strange angles. If the carotid were to leak, the mesh of skin and nylon would never endure the strain of the expanding pocket of blood.

Perhaps he could save her husband, so that the boy wouldn't end up all alone.

And then, just for a moment, he allowed himself a thought that was unacceptable for him: perhaps it might be better if he sabotaged the surgeries, made sure that they all died, all three of them. At least in the afterlife they would remain together. Dawn would come, and it would all be over. The dead would return to where they belonged, and the living would mourn and, in time, forget them. And he would sleep, let his eyelids fall and sleep, let all darken, let the world grow quiet. It would be so easy, nothing much, a couple of cuts, a few slit blood vessels. So many people died every day, what difference would it make if there were a few more? He would be doing them a favour anyway, sparing them so much agony. In the long run, they would be thankful, and they really had no business on this side anyway. This was the side of the living. The dead ought to have known better, ought to have stayed where they were so that the living could continue with their days and nights, with their work and their sleep. Perhaps he could turn them out into the dark, force them across the village boundary, by trickery if need be, so that they could drop there. What a silent, painless end it would be. If only everyone could be so fortunate, blessed with the option to just walk into an invisible wall and disrobe from their skins, walk into the embrace of death, which would welcome the dead, so that the living could go on to live, and rest, and sleep.

It was dreadful, what he was capable of thinking, what he might even be capable of *doing*, just to appease the demons of his exhaustion.

The surgery was done. He undraped the teacher's wife and raised her from her reclining position, supporting the back of her head so that the sutures wouldn't pull. He then wrapped and taped bandages around the neck, around the endotracheal tube, until the neck appeared almost twice its natural thickness. The tube protruded from the front like a proboscis, bobbing under her chin with every movement. He screwed an inflatable bag to the tube's outer end and forced air through it, confirming with his stethoscope that both lungs filled with each puff.

'The less you move your neck, the better. I've stitched the tube in place, so it shouldn't fall out. But be careful. Your ability to breathe will depend on it.'

Then the surgeon busied himself gathering and wiping his instruments so that he wouldn't have to answer her eyes. She sat still, so still, and for so long, while he cleared his trays, that his silence began to feel more and more unacceptable. Since he couldn't bring himself to offer her a prognosis, he just said, 'Come, I've finished. I did what I could.'

Her face appeared taut. 'I'm not afraid of death, Doctor Saheb. Just save my son and my unborn child.'

The walls of the operating room, grey and yellow in the murky light, seemed to close in on the surgeon. He willed the claustrophobia away, wished for it to be replaced with light and air and breath, but he had as little power over this as over anything else. So he just helped the woman down from the table.

Ten

The pharmacist washed the drapes and instruments from the boy's surgery and packed them in a drum that she lowered into the pressure autoclave. After tightening the screws around the edge of the lid, she pressed down a switch on the wall, and a small red light glowed. The temperature gauge was broken, its hand stuck at the fifty-degree mark, so she wet the tip of her finger with her tongue and touched the drum a few times to make sure it was heating as it should. When it began to hiss and steam, she wiped her finger on her dress.

There wasn't much else to do at the moment. Saheb had told her to get some rest while he operated on the boy's mother. She went into the back room and pulled the door shut. After a moment's thought, she slid the latch into place, but slowly, so that the dead wouldn't hear her.

The room held two beds, each a simple frame with a webbing of rusted iron strips holding up an old mattress. The bedsheets were threadbare. She searched the cupboard for better ones, but they were all the same. She picked one that seemed cleaner than the others and spread it out on a mattress. From the pile of blankets in the cupboard, she chose the one at the very bottom. It was quite coarse, and smelled of mothballs, but she, who had washed every conceivable human secretion off these blankets, knew it to be the cleanest.

She lay down on the mattress. The frame creaked so loudly in the still room that she was worried that the iron strips were coming apart under her. With her eyes shut tight, she began to take slow, long breaths to make herself fall asleep. When she found herself lying awake as time drifted by, she blamed the moonlight and the breeze. Rising on one elbow, she closed and shuttered the window and buried her head under the blanket.

Her body felt sore. She tossed on the bed, tried this position and that, but every lump in the mattress seemed to prod her. The pinwheels in her mind showed no sign of slowing down. The more tightly she closed her eyes, the more it seemed that sleep was being squeezed out of them, and the blanket's sickly sweet mothball odour didn't help. She surrendered, threw the blanket off, and stared at the wall at the foot of the bed.

The calendar hanging there had a picture of Goddess Durga printed above the days of the month. When the pharmacist first started working in the clinic, she'd thought of asking her husband to put up a little shelf on that wall, on which she planned to arrange little statuettes of Ganpati and baby Krishna, a picture of Vithoba, maybe one of Sai Baba. But after witnessing Saheb's tantrums at the mention of anything religious, she dropped that plan. The lack of gods in the clinic troubled her, though. In a place that people visited for fear of death, there needed to be *some* source of hope. Then one day it struck her, while strolling through the district market. A calendar with a different god for every month. Twelve gods at the price of one. And Saheb couldn't object to that, could he?

She shuffled to the foot of the mattress and examined the picture, her face inches from the paper. Even in the darkness, she could appreciate Durga's ten hands with their weapons, her large eyes, the lion on which she was seated. The tip of Durga's spear was in the belly of a demon writhing at her feet, his blood splashing on the lion's paws. A violent picture, but the face of the goddess was serene, as if she were barely aware of her victim. Perhaps that's what it was like to be a god – to perform bloody deeds and remain completely untroubled by them.

The calendar was hanging a little crooked on its nail. The pharmacist straightened it and looked around. There was a single spot of light in the room, coming through a hole in the door where there'd once been a doorknob. She'd never been in a position to observe the door from this angle before, with the room darkened and the corridor lit. She left her bed and crept up to the door, placed her eye against the circle, careful not to let the dead see her.

The boy was on the bench, leaning against his father's shoulder. There was a scar on his knee, a little below the point where his short pants ended. It was an old, healed cut, unlike the wounds the three had brought for Saheb to fix. His father was rocking him, humming a lullaby, singing a word once in a while. Why the lullaby, since they couldn't sleep? Was that something the dead did on that plain of theirs – rocked each other and hummed, unable to sleep, unable to stop wanting to sleep?

She stood, looked once again at the calendar, joined her palms in front of her mouth and muttered a few lines of prayer, and then undid the latch and nudged the door open. The man fell silent. The boy raised his head from his father's shoulder and sat straight, as if anxious not to be thought of as a child. She glanced at them out of the corner of her eye, but jerked her head away when she saw them looking back. In all the hours they'd been here, she hadn't been able to bring herself to say a word to them. When the drunkard had appeared, she'd relied on a few frantic gestures to herd them into the back room.

She slipped into the pharmacy, feeling her way in the dark, careful not to dislodge the empty boxes she'd piled so foolishly high on every shelf. One pile almost fell over, and she steadied it, her heart pounding. She inched along the room, feeling the ground with her toe, and stopped when it hit the base of the stone platform at the end. Her eyes had again adjusted to the dark by now, and she lifted the stove that sat atop the platform and gave the tank a quick shake. There was enough kerosene in it. She opened the small bottle of alcohol tucked against the wall. The alcohol spilled as she poured it, but she steadied her trembling hand enough to get a teaspoonful into the spirit cup under the burner. The first match broke in her grip, the next two refused to spark, but with the fourth she managed to light the alcohol. The small flame heated the burner in the centre of the blackened brass rings, and she pumped the drum to get the kerosene flowing. Once the kerosene in the burner was hot enough, it ignited, and blue jets rose from the stove.

The burner made a soft sound, and she sat there a moment, looking at the little roaring ring of fire. In the dark, it seemed to hang in mid-air. And it seemed impossible that something so beautiful and blue could also be so hot. It looked like something she could just scoop up and steal away in her pocket.

She felt under the kitchen platform for the covered bowl she'd left there in the afternoon. It still had some bhendi in it. She scooped half out into a small copper cup and placed it on the flame. The rest she left for Saheb, in case he should want any. She'd also had the good sense to make extra chapatis for lunch that day. She unwrapped two and felt around for some butter to brush onto them, but couldn't remember where she'd kept the can. She didn't want to switch on the light. That would only draw the attention of the dead.

So she put the chapatis, dry as they were, on a plate along with the bhendi, and folded her legs under her on the ground. She held the plate where the thin ribbon of light from the corridor fell across it. Her grandfather used to tell her to chew every morsel thirty-two times, once for each tooth. Only old people ever had time for habits like these, but now seemed as good a time as any to give it a try. With each bite, the bhendi grew more slimy and flavourless. It was missing something, salt perhaps, or ginger, though it had tasted fine that afternoon. But she was hungry, and she wiped the plate clean with the last piece of chapati and rinsed it under a quiet stream in the sink.

There was no reason to expect another attempt at sleep to be more fruitful than the last. So she went into the corridor. The eyes of father and son followed her as she sat on the bench opposite them, her hands pinched between her knees. Above the dead, insects were buzzing against the fluorescent light.

'I—I would have made you something. Some tea at least, and biscuits for the boy. But Saheb said, in your condition, you don't—'

'We don't eat,' said the teacher. 'We don't need food. But thank you. We'll eat again once we're alive, won't we?' He patted his son's shoulder.

'If you need something, just call me. I'll be in—'

'Sorry about—about earlier this evening.'

'About what?'

'When I had to hold you like that. I didn't want to hurt you. I was just afraid you would scream.'

'I did scream. Inside my own mouth.'

The man smiled meekly. 'I hope you aren't afraid of us any longer.'

She tightened her fingers against each other. 'No, I'm not afraid.'

She didn't really have much else to say, and it wasn't clear the teacher did either. She rose.

'Did you study in the city?'

'Me?'

'Your pharmacy training? Was it at the university?'

'I'm not ... not really a pharmacist. I only did seventh standard in school. No training or anything. It's just—there's nobody else here, and Saheb needs someone to look after the place. So my husband and I, we help him take care of it. Saheb registered me as a pharmacist so I could get a salary from the head office.'

'Really? I wouldn't have known. The way you were assisting him during the surgery, it seemed that you knew every instrument, Saheb didn't have to ask twice. How long have you been working for him?'

She sat back on the bench, her ears warm. 'Two and a half years. Since my marriage, when I came to this village. Saheb was looking for someone who could read and write. I don't know English, but Saheb taught me the names of the medicines and instruments. He writes them out, and I practise them every morning. Right after my prayers.'

'And how long has Saheb been here?'

'Six months before me.'

'That's all? Who was here before him?'

'No one. Actually, there was a doctor, but the villagers say he was as good as absent. He visited once every two weeks, wrote something in the account books, and left. The government didn't care, so this went on for many years. And then that doctor disappeared, god knows what happened to him, and Saheb started here. He began to sit in the clinic all day, even when there were no patients.

The villagers didn't know what to think at first. They were afraid he was going to steal their organs and sell them to rich people. Why else would a city doctor come to a village like this? Saheb paid my husband to fix the pipes and the wiring, and then, when I came here after my wedding, he gave me work as well. It looked like an empty godown, this place, the rooms were full of cobwebs. It's so nice now, look.' She pointed at the ceiling so that he could see with his own eyes how clean she kept the corners.

A sharp whistle made her jump, almost fall off the bench. But it was just the autoclave machine. The teacher started at the sound too, as did the boy, but the boy recovered first, and he giggled and poked his father's arm, teasing him for being as scared as a mouse. The pharmacist found herself glancing at their legs.

The teacher wiggled his toes in his slippers. 'No, our feet don't point the other way.'

She brought her hand to her mouth in embarrassment. 'I was just, my mother told me, many years ago—'

'Yes, yes, I know. Ghosts are supposed to leave footprints that point in the wrong direction. Or they're afraid of mirrors, because they don't have a reflection. As if life and death were so simple: just turn one little thing upside down, and the living become dead. All those ghost stories are just that – stories.'

'You can laugh, but they can't *all* be false. I've seen a ghost with my own eyes, I'm telling you. Outside my parents' village, there's a broken-down house. The roof has fallen in, the walls are covered with vines. The man who used to live there, he cheated many women, one after the other – married them with false names and then killed them on the wedding night, can you imagine? He kept doing this – ten times, they say – until the police finally took him off and hanged him. But his wives remained in that house, even after their bodies were burnt and gone. Their souls still roam, looking for some innocent person to haunt, to take revenge for what that demon did to them. I saw one, I swear, once when I was walking back at night a few years ago. I heard a scream that was so loud, my ears kept ringing for days afterwards. There was a woman in a red sari. Her face was white ... whiter than milk, and swollen like a balloon. She was floating in the air, above the roof, and she jumped at me. I ran so fast, I didn't even realize when a piece of glass cut my foot – that's how scared I was. My mother always says there are things in this world that no one can explain.'

She stopped, wondering if she should've told such a gruesome story in front of a child. But the boy didn't seem to mind. He was scratching something into the wood of the bench with a rusted nail he'd found somewhere. Maybe he'd seen worse things himself. She felt it strange that she should be trying to convince the dead of the existence of ghosts, but when she'd finished speaking, the teacher just nodded, his face serious. It seemed that he agreed with her mother. There were things in this world – and, who knew, maybe even the next – that no one could explain.

'I'm sorry you have to be part of all this,' the teacher said. 'To have to deal with us showing up in this state.'

'No, no, I didn't mean it that way. You're not that kind of ghost, I know. And don't worry about me. One night without sleep isn't that bad. Sometimes if we have really sick patients, I stay awake to take care of them.'

A feather blew in through the entrance to the clinic, and the teacher's eyes followed it as it floated all the way to the closed doors of the operating room. His gaze stayed there.

'Everything will work out, with god's mercy,' the pharmacist said.

'I hope so. It's all in Doctor Saheb's hands now.'

'There's nothing Saheb can't fix. So many people come here, so sick, with their legs and stomach so swollen they can't even stand. And then Saheb does his work and in a few days, the men walk out on their own feet. There's nothing he can't cure.'

The man gave a sad smile. 'Has he ever cured death? Brought a corpse to life?'

'Have faith. You're half alive already. Let Saheb worry about the other half.'

The teacher was looking down at his palm, as if reading its lines. The pharmacist took the opportunity to change the subject.

'Did you find out who you were in your past lives?'

When the teacher didn't answer, she said, 'Our family astrologer used to tell us that when we're born, our souls lose their memories. So we live every life as if it were our first. But all of us, we've had many lives before. Hundreds. When we die, we remember all of them. Is that true?'

'Well, I'm—I'm not sure. It might be, but we didn't, at least I didn't, remember any old lives.'

'Oh? Maybe it takes time for those memories to come back.'

'That's possible. Who knows?'

'Our astrologer told me I was a devoted wife in my past life. My husband had an illness in that life that made him bedridden from birth. I served him day and night, washed him and cleaned his sores right up to the end. I don't remember any of this, of course, but the astrologer saw this in the charts he drew up for me. He said that because of my service to my husband, and because I kept away from all sin, from now on I would enjoy the fruits of my good deeds. He told me all this before my engagement, before I had even seen my husband's face, just after the astrologer had checked our horoscopes and told my father that we were destined for each other, lifetime after lifetime. I had forgotten all about it, but I remembered it just now, when we were hiding from that drunkard. What I'm trying to tell you is, I understand tonight why our astrologer took me aside and told me this, though I hadn't even asked him. He must have seen in my charts that a time would come when I would be very scared, that I would want to run away, but it would be a test from God to see if I would serve others in this life just as I did in the last one. The astrologer just wanted me to know that because of my good deeds, nothing would be able to harm me. So I've decided not to be scared. I will help you come back to life, I'll do whatever I can to help Saheb with his work. I know now that I don't need to be afraid of anything, for myself or for my husband.'

All of a sudden, the teacher's lips were trembling and his face looked as though it would crack. The pharmacist wasn't sure what she'd said that could have brought about this change. He started to say something, but then a latch sounded, and the door of the operating room opened. She jumped to her feet, as did the teacher and his son. The man kept his face turned to her, with a look she couldn't read. It was a strange reaction from him, but it lasted just a moment, because then they all ran down the corridor. The surgeon walked out of the operating room, leading the dead woman. Both appeared stiff, as if cut out of cardboard. The pharmacist had to stop herself from gasping at the sight of the neck swollen with bandages.

The teacher touched his wife's arm. 'How are you feeling?'

'Fine.' The woman's face had no expression on it, none at all.

'Are you sure? Was the surgery painful?'

'No. No pain.'

'Careful,' the surgeon said. 'The inner end of that tube is in her windpipe. We'll need it in the morning to ensure that she can breathe.'

The pharmacist wondered if that wouldn't hurt. If a small crumb in the windpipe could make a grown man fall to his knees and choke, wouldn't this plastic thing be much worse? And Saheb wasn't saying anything about how the operation went. Nothing about whether the woman would live. They'd been in the operating room for three hours, and the only things he said now were about the bandages and the tube.

The teacher kept asking his wife, 'Does the tube hurt?' to which she kept saying, her eyes turned away, 'No, it doesn't.' The boy pulled at his mother's fingers, but she avoided his face as well. Though the pharmacist was afraid of what it might be like to touch the dead, she reached out to the boy. She felt his shoulder, skin and bone and soft flesh, there under the shirt, no different than if she'd touched a living child. She kept her fingers there for a few moments, tentatively feeling with their tips, trying to build up the courage to actually rest her entire palm to comfort him, but the boy turned to her with an expression of such anger and annoyance, and shrugged her off so violently, he might as well have slapped her across the face. In an instant, the words she'd just spoken with the dead seemed more remote than the sight of that ghost floating over the house all those years ago. When the surgeon told her to clear out the instruments and replace them with new ones, she was glad to have an excuse to leave the corridor.

She put on a pair of gloves and entered the operating room with a sterilization drum, preparing herself for god alone knew what. The boy's belly had contained so much blood, there'd been a mountain of it at the end of his surgery. It was as if a butcher had sacrificed chickens and goats there and thrown their innards all over the place.

But this time, the drapes were clean. The scalpels and forceps and trays were barely flecked with red. She'd always assumed that the amount of blood spilled said something about how the surgery had gone. But maybe that rule too, like everything else, no longer held with the dead.

She collected the instruments and drapes, washed them in the sink, placed them in layers inside the drum. She peered at the dead through a gap between the doors of the operating room, and then tiptoed to the autoclave machine. The drum inside had now cooled enough for her to reach in and jiggle it loose. As she replaced it with the new one, the surgeon came from the consultation room, carrying a narrow-mouthed glass jar with a rubber lid, half filled with water. She'd seen the jar in the cupboard, she'd dusted around it before, but there was something different about it now. Yes, Saheb had made two holes in the lid, and stuck plastic tubes through them.

He took the sterilized drum from her, pushed the door of the operating room open with his foot, and waited there with his back to everyone else. 'It's my turn now,' the teacher said to his wife and son, and the door closed behind the two men.

Only mother and son were left on the bench under the fluorescent light. The pharmacist stayed at the end of the corridor. The bulb in the ceiling above her had burnt out. She felt like a ghost herself, hidden in the shadows, spying on the dead.

The boy's eyes were on his mother's neck, on the tube sticking out at the front.

'Doctor Saheb said this is to help you breathe. Is that true?'

'That's what he says, so it must be true.'

'Why did he put this tube in you and not me?'

'Because my neck is hurt. The air we breathe passes through the throat, right here.'

'Will Baba need a tube too?'

'I don't know. We'll find out soon, after his surgery is done.'

'Does this mean that without the tube you wouldn't be able to breathe?'

'Saheb's just being careful.'

'And is it fixed now?'

'I'm sure it is.'

The boy didn't seem satisfied with her answers. He folded his arms and sat back with a sullen pout.

The pharmacist remained flattened against the wall, her shoulders aching from the effort of concealment. The autoclave machine whispered beside her instead of making its usual whistling sound. Was the seal not tight enough? She moistened her finger on her tongue and pressed it to the lid.

The heat was like an electric shock. She bit down on the scream that tried to burst through her throat. Tears squeezed from her eyes as she pressed her fist shut to numb the finger.

The boy was saying something. She ignored the burn. They still hadn't noticed her.

He had snuggled close to his mother. 'Aai, I want to taste food again.'

'Yes.' The woman's voice broke. 'I want to cook for you. When we're all well and healed, I will cook you the best food I've ever cooked.'

'Will you cook me mutton?'

'Yes, my baby, I will. I'll cook it just as you like it – spicy, and with plenty of coconut.'

'And will you make me solkadhi?'

'Yes, I'll make you solkadhi, as sour as you want it to be.'

'And we'll have mango pulp?'

'Yes, fresh mangoes. You can drink the pulp till your stomach is full, so full that you'll fall asleep at your plate and I'll have to wash your hands and mouth and carry you to bed.'

The woman folded her arms around her son and looked out through the doorway of the clinic. She seemed to be pleading with someone, with God perhaps, or the stars.

Her son rested his head on her pregnant belly. 'After we come back to life, what if we die again?'

'Why are you asking that, my baby?' She combed away a twig stuck in his hair with her finger.

'What if someone attacks us, and this happens again?'

'It won't happen, I promise. Those were bad people, but they're far away now.'

'But aren't there any bad people in this village? What if they don't want us here?'

'Don't say that, my child. Most people aren't like that. Most people are kind, they want to help others, even strangers.'

'But not all. How do we find out who the bad people are?'

'God will keep us safe. He'll protect us.'

'And will the angel protect us?'

'Yes, I'm—I'm sure he will. Baba has great faith in him.'

The woman sat that way for a while, looking down at the side of her son's face, and then her eyes moved to the village beyond the hillock.

'That looks like a school,' she said. 'That's where you'll study, and that's where Baba will work too.'

'Will we ever go back to our house?'

'We can never leave this village, no matter what happens, you know that. Maybe when you're older you'll understand this better, but for now you have to trust your father and me. You can never cross the boundary of this village, not even for a second. Not even if there's a pile of gold and diamonds on the other side.'

'But where will we live?'

'Saheb is generous. He'll help us. I'm sure the villagers will help too. It won't be easy – we won't have any money, and we'll have to live on what others give us. But you're a big boy now. I know you won't be stubborn if you don't get everything you want. Someday we'll have our own house. Right here, at the foot of this hill.'

The boy pointed at something. 'Is that a temple?' The pharmacist could see it from where she stood, and yes, a pennant fluttered above it in the moonlight. The boy had a good eye.

'Maybe. It looks like one,' said his mother. 'We'll go there to pray every morning. Those white flowers you like, we'll make garlands out of them. I wonder what kind of statues they have. I hope they're made of stone, I like those better than the metal—'

The boy stood up and held his face against his mother's, pressed his forehead and nose to hers, his left cheek to her right. 'I'll take care of you, Aai. I know you're really hurt, but I'll take care of you.'

His mother cupped his cheeks in her hands. 'I know you will, my baby, I know you will.' She pulled him to her breast.

The pharmacist, as she watched this from the end of the corridor, couldn't help but feel that there was something strange about the woman's face, something unnatural, though she wasn't quite sure what it was. Then a drop rolled down her own cheek, and she realized. The woman's eyes were as dry as paper. They remained dry while she rocked her son back and forth, though her chest shook with sobs. So the pharmacist let her own eyes spill, drop by drop, what the woman strained to spill but could not, for flowing tears, like flowing blood, were denied to the dead.

Eleven

Even when they were in the operating room and the door was closed, the teacher did not ask, 'Will she live?' and so the surgeon did not answer, 'I don't think she will.' The man just took off his shirt and raised himself onto the operating table, and the surgeon put his stethoscope to his ears.

On the right side of the chest – the side of the stabbing – the surgeon couldn't hear any air filling the lung. When he tapped in the spaces between the ribs, the cavity rang dull under his fingers, as if he were tapping on stone.

'You bled into your chest. How long was the blade?'

The teacher held his thumb and forefinger about six inches apart. The surgeon looked at the wound, and the teacher brought his outstretched fingers close to his chest in response. With the thumb placed against the gash, his forefinger curved all the way along the rib to the breastbone. A knife that size, driven to the hilt, could have hit anything. The surgeon scratched his stubble, kneaded a knot in his jaw with his thumb.

He had the teacher lie on his side, facing away, his right arm folded up over his head. He picked up the razor he'd left on the shelf. Strands of hair still clung to it, long, fine hair from the back of the woman's head. He unscrewed and washed the razor, snapped on a new blade. With it, he carefully shaved the man's armpit and part of his right chest, clearing a broad margin around the wound. Then he scrubbed the chest with iodine and covered the upper and lower areas with drapes, leaving only a strip of skin exposed at the level of the injury.

'Hold your breath.'

The chest under the drapes stopped moving. The surgeon put his scalpel to the skin and extended the wound in both directions – towards the breastbone alone the line of the rib, and backward, first under the shoulder blade and then curving upward along the spine. The teacher's arm was raised, and his skin was stretched. The edges of the new incision parted as soon as the scalpel passed through them.

'There was a palmist at the village fair,' said the teacher. His chest did not move. He too could speak without having to breathe.

'Um?'

'Sorry. I can keep quiet if you'd prefer—'

'No, go ahead. What were you saying?'

'At the fair, on the day this happened, we had our palms read.'

'Really? You believe in that kind of thing?'

'Not me, Saheb, no. But my wife used to. Who knows, maybe she still does, even after everything.'

'And what did the palmist tell you?'

'That all three of us had perfect lifelines, stretching all the way to our wrists. Not a single break.'

'You should ask for your money back.'

'He was sitting on a mat, Saheb, under a tattered umbrella for shade. He had these dusty signboards around him, with drawings of palms and lines and numbers.'

'And you took pity on him?'

'His clothes were torn. He looked old and tired ... probably hadn't eaten much that day. People were walking by without even noticing him. It was just a few rupees, and he spoke to my son as lovingly as he would've to his own grandchild.'

'Well, it's all a question of the right setting,' said the surgeon. 'Sit an old man on a mat, and no one looks his way. Put him in a clinic, and even angels refer him patients.'

He had finished cutting through the fat under the man's skin. He pulled aside the fleshy muscle that ran across the surface of the rib cage and cut through others, careful not to injure the nerves in the region. He then sliced through the muscles that held together the ribs flanking the wound, right down to the pleura on the inside of the ribs. He used to have a rib retractor, but the pharmacist had dropped and broken it over a year ago, and he hadn't felt the need to purchase another. So he just pulled the ribs apart with his hands, as though he were prying open the bony lips of a cavernous maw. The interior of the chest was as he'd expected.

'It's full of blood.'

'Can it be fixed?'

'Don't know that yet.'

If the heart had been punctured, or one of the arteries around it, this was the end. There was absolutely nothing here that would allow him to repair that. But there was just too much blood. Litres of it, from what he could estimate, obscuring everything.

The teacher's face was turned away from the surgeon, half covered by the edge of the drape. It was clear the man wasn't feeling any pain, but the surgeon now wondered if he had any sensation at all, any awareness of what part of him the scalpel was cutting at a given moment. Maybe one could pluck out every organ, disjoint the bones, reduce the man to just a head, then trim even that down – the cheeks, the lips, the tongue. Would words still issue from a bare skull?

'These villagers are lucky, Saheb.'

'Are they?'

'How many villages have someone like you, someone with your skill? There's so much money to be made in cities, but still, here you are, serving the poor.'

The surgeon had begun to clean out the interior of the chest, and found that it wasn't easy holding the ribs apart and digging out clots at the same time without a retractor or an assistant. Removing one of the ribs to make some space wasn't a bad thought, but it would probably be more trouble than it was worth. It was a mercy the man was thin. No roll of fat around his chest to force apart every time.

'There are very few people like you, Saheb, who willingly sacrifice their comforts for others. Everyone's just concerned with their own lives, interested in adding to their wealth. All greed and selfishness.'

The teacher paused, considered his own words.

'But what right do I have to judge anyone else? I want life, don't I? Life on earth, even after my death. The one thing that no one's really supposed to have. Maybe that's real greed, worse than wanting money or fame.'

The surgeon smiled. 'Philosophy is for the elderly. You're much too young for thoughts like these. Leave them to people my age.'

'But don't they say that philosophy is for those who struggle with death? If that's true, who could be more qualified than me?'

The cuffs and sleeves of the surgeon's gown were a deep red by now. The sides of the incision closed over his forearm each time he reached in, and a wet, sucking sound accompanied every handful of clots he pulled out. They came in clumps and threads – dark, shiny, teasing their way free through his gloves. Try as he did, he couldn't keep some of them from slipping to the floor. He would have to remember to clean them off later, or the whole clinic would be smeared.

'My son's feet ached,' the teacher said. 'He wanted to take a rickshaw home from the fair, and I teased him, "You're a big boy, you should be able to walk, it isn't that far."'

'Don't say that. It wasn't your fault. You shouldn't blame yourself.'

'If only I'd listened to him, Saheb, if only I'd taken a minute to stop and think. It was getting dark. My wife shouldn't have been walking in her state anyway. But I wasn't thinking. I just wasn't thinking.'

It was clear where this conversation was headed. The surgeon thought of enforcing silence on the teacher, under the pretence of medical requirement if need be. But the time when he could have done so came and went, and the man just kept speaking. The surgeon pulled his hand out from between the ribs and placed his bloody glove on the cloth covering the teacher's shoulder. He knew full well that the man would feel this gesture as little as he did the cuts and tugs on his insides.

'They twisted my arms behind my back, Saheb. Held me as if I were nothing more than a child. They started pulling off our valuables. "Take everything," I begged them. "Take her mangalsutra, her bangles. Take my ring, my watch. My wallet has a week's pay. Take it. We won't fight, won't make a sound." And still the knives, Saheb. Why?

'I could see their teeth. They were smiling. And then this pain ... I'd never felt pain like this. Every single breath, it felt as if someone were tearing out my ribs. My wife's clothes were covered with blood. My son was on the ground, he was holding his stomach, "Baba, I'm hurt, I'm hurt." The men had already run away. Imagine me, Saheb, trying to breathe, trying to stop her bleeding. It kept flowing through my fingers, hot as boiling water. Imagine, Saheb, her face all red, her eyes rolled back, and my child ... *our* child, our baby, ready to be born ...

we even had names for it, one if it was a boy, another if a girl, dying inside her, and I could do nothing. I couldn't even kneel there and cry. My son was screaming behind me, so I left her. She was gone. There was nothing I could do, so I left her.

'His shirt was wet. I grabbed his arms, dragged him – my boy whom I used to swing over my back but whom I couldn't even lift off the ground now. Who knows how long we went like this ... it was so dark, the street was swaying from side to side, it was as if I were walking on a rope. So I fell. What lies I whispered in his ears then. "Don't be afraid, help is coming, I'm here with you." Yes, I was there with him, Saheb, as nothing but a witness. My boy stopped breathing in my arms, and I could do nothing. May this never happen to any father, Saheb, may no one ever have to feel what I felt. I tried to scream, but there was no air left in my lungs. And who was there to listen? I felt only hate, nothing but hate. And my greatest hatred wasn't even for the bandits. It was for that palmist at the fair. That poor old man, he had done nothing to hurt us, but as the pressure in my chest became unbearable, and the next breath became impossible to take, I could only think of his promises, about our lifelines and how long they were supposed to be. And then I died.'

The man spoke in a smothered voice, as if he were strangling himself with restraint. The surgeon could only see the side of his face, not even that, really, just his ear and the back of his cheek. The rest was either covered by the drape or in shadow. There was no consolation fit for such an unburdening, and so a silence fell between them. Something as raw and horrific as this, the surgeon couldn't bring himself to scrape at it with words.

'We've suffered so much, Saheb. I feel so terrible about all the trouble we're putting you through, putting the girl and her husband through, but please understand, we've suffered so much.'

The surgeon loosened his grip on the shoulder and searched again between the ribs. The clots the man's chest surrendered were as gruesome as his words, but at least the surgeon knew what to do with them. He scooped them over to a tray, shook them off his fingers.

Then he said, 'I'm not here to serve the poor.'

The teacher turned ever so slightly towards him. His eyelashes caught the light from the anglepoise lamp.

'I've been here, in this village, for almost three years, and every single day I've thought of just packing up and leaving. It would be dishonest of me to let you think otherwise.'

The teacher's face remained where it was, his eyes turned in the surgeon's direction without actually looking at him.

'I used to practise in a large private hospital in the city. We had conveniences there – luxuries compared to this place – that I would barely even notice. New instruments, imported machines, trained nurses. I just assumed I would have all of those resources until I retired – all I had to do was snap my fingers.

'And then one day one of my patients became unstable

after a surgery. I did everything I could, but he kept worsening, and the patient's family demanded that he be shifted elsewhere. The hospital they wanted was at the other end of the city. Late that night, an ambulance managed to get him there alive.

'I called early the next morning to find out how things had gone. The staff at that hospital told me that the patient was in the operating room, undergoing a second, emergency surgery. I asked them who was operating, and they told me the surgeon's name.

'It was a man who'd worked in the same hospital as me. Actually he'd been my subordinate – this was a decade earlier. He was a terrible surgeon – lazy and impatient, bothered only about getting through his quota of cases for the shift and going home. Neglecting so many details that he would routinely put patients' lives in danger. I had to fix so many of the problems he caused that finally I had him fired. It had been ten years since I'd even thought of him. And now here he was, operating on my patient.

'When the surgery was finally done, they connected me to him. I could hear it over the phone – his triumph – from his very first word, from the way he greeted me. He asked about the old hospital, about how things were, how the other doctors and matrons and ward boys were doing, pretending he had no idea why I'd called. He had been operating since dawn, but there wasn't a trace of tiredness in his voice.

'I let this go on for some time and then asked about the patient. As if tossing off a minor detail, he said, "Oh, he's going to die." And then he told me he'd identified a surgical error when he opened the man up. I had cut something I shouldn't have cut, he said, tied a vessel I shouldn't have tied.

'I racked my brain, tried to remember every minute of the surgery, every suture and knot, but I just couldn't believe I'd done as he claimed. I kept questioning his findings, hoping to clarify some detail that would prove him wrong. I asked to speak to one of the surgeons who'd assisted him, to see if that person had the same opinion of the case. That's when his voice changed.

'"I don't have time," he said, "for fools who can't accept their own mistakes."

'It was reasonable that he would want revenge, I understand that now. I was a fool, yes, and like a fool I tried to reason with him. We'd worked together. He knew me, he knew how careful I was. I was just requesting him to consider this a special case.

'"A special case?" he said. "Really? Well, if that's so, let's see how special you're willing to make it. I'm open to changing my report. Assuming you're willing to reach an arrangement. Five lakh rupees. I don't need to tell you there won't be a receipt."

'I'd been lucky until then, I have to say. I'd managed to get very far in life without being forced into a corner like this. If it took six extra months to get a telephone line installed, that was fine, I could deal with it. If a hundred other people paid under the table to move things along faster, best of luck to them. But I'd never dreamed that this would happen ... that I'd be blackmailed for a mistake I couldn't even remember making.

'I yelled into the phone, cursed him and his kind – termites hollowing out every institution. But every word I spoke just gave him more power over me. He was only trying to help me, he said. It'd be easy. All I had to do was take a briefcase to my bank and then bring it to him. "Don't try to complicate simple things," he said. "And don't try to negotiate me down, I'm not some jewellery salesman."

'"You're nothing *but* a jewellery salesman," I shouted, "trying to hawk some diamond you've dug out of a corpse. Buying a new Mercedes, are you? How many bribes is that going to take? I hope your mother isn't alive to see this. If she'd known what kind of snake you'd turn out to be, she wouldn't have let your father fuck her in the first place."

'The man disconnected. I kept calling, but he wouldn't answer, and in the evening, I learnt from a nurse that the patient had died—'

The surgeon felt a wetness on his forearm. He yanked his arm out of the teacher's chest, tugged at the knot at his waist, tore off his gown. A red band circled his wrist above the level of the glove. He turned the tap in the sink on full, but only a sluggish stream came out. Under it, he scrubbed a bar of soap into a pink froth. The water's ropy pressure was excruciatingly gentle. He had to hold his skin against the tap to coax the foam down into the drain.

Blood, it was just blood. The little that had soaked through his sleeve. It was harmless. It wasn't acid, it wouldn't corrode his flesh. Nor were the dead branding him as one of their own with some demonic ink. The surgeon gripped the porcelain rim with his dripping hands to hold the world steady. The water reached from the mouth of the tap to the floor of the sink in a thin, silent column. Every so often, it would lose its inner harmony, and a gurgle from the spout would scatter the glassy stream.

The surgeon let the thudding in his chest fade. Then he shut the tap, gowned and gloved again, returned to the table. The teacher's face was blank. Without comment, the surgeon dipped into the man's open chest again, with greater care for his scrubs this time. The teacher did not react to that either. It was clear he was waiting for the story to resume.

The surgeon sighed. 'I've often thought about that conversation. Maybe, at the bottom of all this, his findings were real, and I was too conceited to accept them. After all, it had been a routine surgery for a minor condition. The patient was otherwise in perfect health. Maybe I *was* at fault, and deserved to be fined.

'What happened was much worse. The surgeon released the most incriminating report he could possibly write. He filled it with accusing words, speculations about my skills, things that definitely didn't belong there. But who can stop an author determined to write a tragedy? And that wasn't even the worst thing. Then he called the press. And told them I'd tried to bribe him.

'There were no riots that week, no activists going on hunger strikes; so, every news agency descended on his hospital. The bastard told them that I'd offered him money to keep his mouth shut. But he couldn't be bought, not he, with his conscience bathed in milk. Not even if I gave him a Mercedes. He must have emphasized that word, *Mercedes,* to every reporter, for it was used in every article. I imagine he wanted to make sure I read it.

'His accusation shattered my life. The telephone company released records of the calls I'd dialled – proof that I'd made all those frantic attempts to contact him. The resident who'd assisted in the surgery was a timid young man, and when the police questioned him, he just repeated everything his superior had said. My name was blackened in every newspaper in the city. Headline news, daily updates, rumours – my photo next to murderers and rapists.

'After two weeks of this, I was summoned by the head of the department. "I sympathize with your position," he said. "Patients sometimes die from our mistakes, and we as doctors have to accept that possibility. But the public doesn't see it that way. They expect us to be perfect. And above everything else, they expect us to be honest. Exemplary citizens. All that bullshit."

'By that point, he didn't care if the operative report was true. Nor if the claim of bribery was true. He was answerable to the trustees of the hospital, and they to the public. Someone had to be sacrificed, and it wouldn't be him. As I signed my letter of resignation, he asked why I hadn't come to him earlier. He knew people in the press, he said. He could've paid them to hold their tongues.

'The compensation the court made me pay wiped my savings away. It wasn't just for medical negligence – the accusation of bribery made the penalty ten times higher. I'm still astonished that my lawyer managed to save me from a prison sentence. No hospital would dream of hiring me now. Corruption, the secret friend of everyone from the top to the bottom of the chain, was a landmine when the world was looking. I had no money to open my own clinic. No bank would give me a loan, and no one would have referred me any patients anyway. So I left the city, at my age, and came to work in this government clinic. The villagers respect me because they don't know my past. The government knows everything, of course, but it's better to fill a clinic like this with a disgraced doctor than with cobwebs.

'So there it is. It's a long story, but after everything you've been through, you don't deserve any more lies. I just want you – I need you – to understand that I'm not a saint. And I'm certainly not God. If you mistake me for either, you'll be very disappointed, I promise you.'

Only as the surgeon neared the end of his tale did he truly realize he was delivering it to a patient, and to one so young. But the chasm between them – the living and the dead – had already made all earthly hierarchies seem pointless.

For a long time, the teacher remained quiet. Once or twice, he made as if to say something. When he finally did speak, it seemed to take him some effort to control his voice.

'Doctor Saheb, how does it matter if we think of you as God or man? When we were dying on the roadside, no one came to our help. No man, no God. For us, you are more than either. We're thankful for whatever you can do for us, and we won't have any complaint, no matter how this should end. I can only apologize again for everything, for all the trouble we're causing you.'

The man's chest had finally been emptied of blood. A shrunken lung was crushed deep inside it. Behind it, the heart hid like a timid animal that had retreated into the depths of its cave. There was no flowing blood to inflate it, but it still appeared to have a beat, or, more precisely, a throb. It shivered under the surgeon's fingers, as though in fear or yearning for the moment when it would once again be entrusted with life.

The light was miserable, and even with the ribs propped apart with an improvised retractor, the lamps lit only a sliver of the interior brightly enough. Most of the cavity remained dark. There was a small battery torch on the windowsill, but it wasn't sterile. The surgeon wondered if it was worth spraying it with alcohol and holding it in one hand while he examined the interior of the chest with the other, but he decided against it. He would never be able to get it acceptably clean. So he just started feeling with his fingers, inch by inch, along the surface of every structure that could possibly have been the source of the bleed.

'Tell me, why do you want to come back? Some day or the other, all of us have to die and end up in the afterlife, don't we? So why endure this anxiety, the uncertainty of this night?'

The teacher's eyes were fixed on the far wall. He was following, it seemed, an ant meandering up the tiles. So the fumigation hadn't accomplished anything after all, had it? But the surgeon felt no anger towards the black dot. The hapless little thing – even it had the right to live, on this night when the dead themselves were being smuggled across the border. It crawled across the cracked tile and vanished into the grime at its edge.

'We were murdered. My son deserves a full life.'

'Yes, yes, you've said that before, but that isn't everything, is it? You're hiding something.'

The teacher's ribs now moved for the first time in quite a while. The motion didn't disturb the surgeon, so he let the man breathe.

'When I first told you about the afterlife, Saheb, I was careful with my words. For the sake of my son. I would like to think he's still a child – that I have some control over what he should and shouldn't know. Or believe.'

'Yes, but he's not here now. You can speak openly.'

'But, Saheb, it's not supposed to be this way, the living aren't supposed to learn about the afterlife. Please understand, I don't want to hide anything from you, but there are some things you might be better off not knowing.'

'And why do you think you have the right to decide what to keep from me?'

The teacher appeared wounded by the question. He straightened the arm that was folded under his head, and let it stick out from beneath the drapes, over the edge of the operating table.

'The afterlife is a barren place. There's no valley or mountain to catch your eye. Every direction looks like every other. You could walk up and down it forever, and so many have – the dead who don't even know why they're wandering any more. Who would want to live in a place like that, Saheb? It's like being exiled to a desert. Worse. All we can do there is wander, hope that relief will come if we walk just a little bit more, find some magical resting place. Our legs don't get tired, we don't need food or sleep. But the soul, it gets tired. It wants to *feel* something, even pain.'

'But that doesn't answer my question. You, all three of you, could live here till you're old and bent, and after everything's done, you'll still end up there. So how is this, all the suffering you'll have to face at dawn, how is any of this worth it?'

'It will be worth it, Saheb, I'm telling you. The suffering will be temporary, it will go away, and then we'll be able to feel things again, all the little things that we can only feel on earth. I want to drink water again, Saheb – ice-cold water. Sometimes I imagine it's collecting on my tongue, that I can roll it against my teeth, feel it in the bones of my head, smell it – water has smell, I never realized that before my death – and then feel it in my throat when I swallow, that feeling right here in my chest, spreading outwards, rib after rib, down to my stomach ... I know I must sound half-mad when I talk like this, but it's these things that really separate life from death. Yes, I'll have to return someday, but now that I know what it's like, the time I spend on earth will be different. I know the value of every breath. I will live a life in which I teach others to appreciate it, help them lead better lives themselves. Maybe even become a farmer, grow my own food so that I know what it's like to sow life into the soil. All of these things ... maybe they'll help me tolerate the afterlife better when I return.'

The surgeon grimaced. It was too naïve, all of this. Not what he'd expected at all, certainly not from someone whose knowledge of life was supposed to surpass his own.

'Fine, but why not just wait until it's your turn to be reborn? Through a woman's womb? Why this plan to return in the middle of the night?'

The rapture that had entered the teacher's voice at the talk of water now drained out of it just as quickly. 'I don't believe it, Saheb. I don't think anyone is ever reborn. Everyone talks about it in the afterlife. In fact, that's all they talk about. But I ... I don't believe it.'

'But didn't you say that your angel told you about it? Or were you lying to me?'

'Not lying, Saheb. Please understand, I just said what I did for my son's sake. All useless, I'm sure. My boy has seen so much – all it takes is a moment in the afterlife, and children remain children no more. But what else can a father do?'

'Get to the point.'

'The angel isn't an angel. He's an official of the afterlife.'

The surgeon stopped dead in his work. 'An official?'

'Yes. One of the many who run the afterlife.'

'I don't understand. Officials? The afterlife is run by *officials*?'

'Yes. It's all based on the promise of rebirth. Everyone needs hope, Saheb – the dead as much as the living. So they pray to the officials, who are said to be the gatekeepers.'

'What—what are you saying?'

'That's how it starts, Saheb – appeals and rejections, rejections and appeals. The officials have different conditions for rebirth. Some say our lives are important, others our deaths. Some go through our sins, other talk about our penance. Every thought, every word we've ever said – things we did as children, before we even knew right from wrong – we are forced to justify it all until we have no dignity left. But nothing ever satisfies the officials. They say they need to think about it, they need to check with their superiors. They tell us they'll return when they've reached a decision, and we never see them again.'

A crow, perhaps the insomniac from earlier in the night, cawed outside the window, and the night wind drew a soft rattle from the shutters.

'So you're saying the afterlife is like a bureaucracy? A government bureaucracy?'

'Much worse. No government on earth could create a bureaucracy like this. It's endless. There are probably more officials in the afterlife than there are dead people. The reason the three of us are here, the reason I'm telling you all this, Saheb, is that one official was different, and we were lucky enough to find him. Our story moved him, I don't know why. We had nothing to offer him, but still he decided to break his laws for us. Please, Saheb, don't tell my son these things. He's just a child. He deserves to grow up with some hope about life, maybe even about death.'

The surgeon just stood, forearm-deep in the teacher's ribs. Because he had to do something, he tried to return to his work, but his hands kept falling still. The insane turn of the teacher's narration wouldn't let him focus, nor would the patina of sleep that, despite everything, kept building over his eyes. How much of the teacher's account had truly come from the man's lips, and how much had his own brain fabricated in its exhaustion? He was now passing his fingers in an unending circuit inside the man's chest, but he still wasn't sure that the large vessels hadn't been harmed. The walls had gained a darker tint, and it seemed that the door and windows of this shuttered room would never open again. The two of them – the dead and the living – would continue this conversation until the tiles blackened and crumbled.

'Is there a God?' the surgeon asked.

The teacher turned to the wall.

'Answer my question. You've been talking about all these officials, but not about gods.'

The very act of speech seemed to age the teacher, making him softer and hoarser. 'In the afterlife, we called out to God. We recited every prayer we had ever learnt. We searched so desperately that any God with a drop of kindness in Him would have come to us ... at least shown us some sign. But He didn't. God is as hidden to the dead as He is to the living.'

There was a coldness on the surgeon's face, on the back of his arms. But it wasn't from the teacher's words. The surgeon could now feel a hole under his fingers. In the vena cava, right where the vessel entered the heart. How could this be? Surely he'd checked the spot before. Had he himself poked a hole through it with his prodding? No, no, that wasn't possible. The vessel was in the path of the stabbing. The knife could very well have hit it. The hole didn't even appear to have a flap in front of it. There was nothing to stitch back into place. He pulled his hand out to take a look.

The teacher just kept speaking. 'There are religions in the afterlife, Saheb. Just not the ones from earth. Even those who were faithful believers in life have to wonder how their priests and holy books could have been so wrong. But that has only led to new religions, made by stitching together shreds of the older ones. Some of the dead claim to be prophets and sages – men of God. They say they can hear His voice, that they want to spread His words to everyone who hopes to be reborn. I don't understand what they get out of this. There's no money or land or gold to gather there. Maybe it's just the sense of power.'

No, it wasn't a hole. It was just another clot – a piece that had flattened and plastered itself against the vena cava so that it seemed to the surgeon's numb fingers like a portion of the wall itself. He had to stop obsessing over this. It would kill him if he kept looking for false alarms in the dark. The large vessels were fine.

But what could explain the chest full of blood? Not that little rent in the lung?

The small vessels running in the groove under the rib's edge were difficult to examine. The angle of light was completely wrong. The knife could very well have cut them, but he'd run his fingers over that area and hadn't felt anything suspicious. There was really no way to improve the positions of the lamps, so he asked the teacher to turn sideways, arch to the left, and inflate his rib cage as far as it would go so the groove under the rib could catch the light. As the man repositioned himself, the wound, framed by its green drapery, opened and closed like a carnivorous plant smacking its blood-flecked jaws after a feast. It took a few tries, but the man finally contorted himself into a pose that offered a reasonable view.

The artery and vein were so collapsed that it wasn't even clear which was which in the groove of the rib. And there was no spurting blood to act as a guide. The surgeon brushed his finger over the inner curve of the rib, but couldn't find a cut. Maybe it was best to assume that one of the vessels was the culprit, and close them off by tying blind knots on either side of the injury. He started to dissect what appeared to be the artery and vein away from what was probably the nerve.

'What did your angel, your official, say? Didn't you ask him about God?'

'I did, but he didn't answer. He didn't like to talk about these things.'

'And didn't you ask him how all of this came into existence? The afterlife? The system of officials?'

'My official wouldn't say anything about that either; but there was a wanderer I met, Saheb, a very strange man. He said he'd once been an official. He told me—'

'Once been an official? How do you know he wasn't lying?'

'I don't. I'm mentioning him only because he told me something that might answer your question. As an official, he'd been assigned to a province, he said. He kept an eye on things, recorded births and deaths. It was boring work, so he decided to play with his subjects. He took the form of a celestial messenger and appeared on earth—'

'In person?'

'Yes. He told me that he made his skin glow, just like a firefly. It was a simple trick for him, but it was enough to make any human who saw him drop to his knees. He appeared before a few men, told them that God was willing to offer them great powers if they could please Him with their devotion. The men all left their wives and children, went into caves, ate only seeds and roots, and spent their days in meditation. Some of them almost starved to death.

'So the official thought, why stop there? He started granting the powers he'd promised. To one man he gave the strength of ten elephants. To another he taught a spell to create fire from air. A third he gave the ability to cause agony with a glance. Awful things happened, and the official watched them, entertained.

'But he wasn't careful. After the men had taken revenge on their neighbours, they started intimidating people in other towns, threatened to kill them and their children if they didn't bow to them. That's when other officials began to notice these monsters with abilities that no human was supposed to have. The official tried to cover things up by killing his creations, but it was too late. He was discovered and exposed. His superiors judged him guilty, took away his authority and powers, and sentenced him to the worst punishment possible – permanent exile on the plain of the dead, as one of its wanderers.

'Whether this man was telling me the truth, or if he was just another one of us, a madman before he died or someone driven mad by the afterlife, I don't know. He said he had reflected on his actions, he'd changed, repented. Now he only wished to spread the truth. And so he told me that the officials themselves don't really know if God exists. They have a hierarchy, like a ladder, with steps that go on and on, the lower officials reporting to the higher ones and so forth. No one knows who's at the very top. No one even knows if the ladder ever ends.'

The surgeon tied a knot under the teacher's rib and made two snips with his scissors. He then pulled out the segment of tissue, stretched it between his fingers, held it to the light. One of the cords, likely the artery, had a cut in its wall, right where the knife would be expected to have grazed it. It was tiny, but sufficient in the right situation to pump a man's chest full of blood. The surgeon kept turning it over, let the light glint off its neat rectangular shape until he was finally convinced that he'd repaired the fatal injury. Then he searched within himself for the slightest trace of relief. He could find none.

He used two rows of stitches to close the rent in the surface of the lung. A separate puncture, lower in the rib cage, would be needed for the drainage tube. He made a cut in the skin at the edge of a lower rib, and tunnelled the puncture through to the inside, taking care not to injure the diaphragm. He threaded the chest tube from the outside of the chest to the space between the lung and the ribs, and once its tip was high enough in the thorax, he secured the outer portion to the skin with loops of sutures. After confirming that it was anchored in place, he drew the ribs back together and sutured the muscles between them. Then it was time to close the other layers of the chest wall – the muscles, the connective tissue, the skin. Once the drapes were lifted off, the incision with its closed lips made a macabre smile that stretched across the side of the chest. He dressed it with gauze and tape.

He now had the teacher sit up. Their eyes met, and the surgeon narrowed his and looked down at the man's neck in a pretence of clinical scrutiny. He'd forgotten where he'd left the glass jar, and he looked around until the teacher pointed to the stone shelf jutting from the wall. The surgeon adjusted the plastic tubes passing through the jar's lid so that the inner end of one of the tubes was submerged in the water, while the other ended an inch above the surface. To the outer end of the submerged tube he attached longer, flexible tubing, and into the other end of this tubing he twisted the end of the chest tube sticking out of the man's ribs. The tubes fit into each other neatly. After confirming that the seal around the rubber lid was tight, he asked the teacher to cough. Air gushed through the piping and bubbled to the water's surface.

'You'll have to carry this jar around with you. It's sturdy, but don't drop it. Take care not to tilt or spill it either – the end of that tube has to remain under water, no matter what. Hold this glove to your mouth, and inflate it like a balloon repeatedly for the next hour. That'll generate enough pressure to inflate your lungs. There's a lot of air outside them, in the space where all that blood had collected. The air will bubble out as the lung expands to its original shape.'

He'd kept his watch on his wrist during this surgery, and it told him now that it was a little after four in the morning. Less than two hours to sunrise. Somehow, in the hour and a half since they'd entered the operating room, the teacher hadn't brought up the one thing the surgeon had feared he would. Then, when asked to step down from the table, the man asked, 'Will she live?' The only answer the surgeon could give was, 'I don't think she will.' The teacher folded his face into his hands. Even through the walls of the room, the surgeon could feel the pressure of the heavy sky, and of everything beyond it.

Twelve

The pharmacist leaned against the entrance of the clinic, waiting for the sound of a bicycle, waiting for the night to return her husband. The boy sat on the steps, examining a pile of boxes a few feet away. The boxes were rustling. He aimed a pebble at one, and a rat ran out from underneath it. With a small ball of cotton as its loot, it fled into its burrow and hid somewhere in the clinic walls.

The boy's mother was on the bench, her back pressed against the wall and her head set straight on her neck. She was still in the tattered green gown she'd worn for the surgery. A safety pin held the neckline together. The bandages were a thick white wrap above the gown.

She called out to him without turning, 'Don't do that, my baby. Don't damage those boxes.'

'No problem, really,' the pharmacist said. 'I was going to throw them out anyway. He can play with them if he wants.'

The boy chose a box made of thermocol.

The pharmacist knelt next to him. 'Do you ... did you go to school?'

'Yes.' He began carving pieces of the box away with a thumbnail.

'And what standard were you studying in?'

The boy climbed down the steps and returned with some twigs from the mud. 'Third standard.'

'How nice. You're such a big boy. Did your father teach you in school?'

'No, he taught the ninth and tenth standards.' He pressed the twigs into the squares he'd carved in the thermocol.

She clapped her hands in delight. 'You're making a house.'

'It's not a house.' He placed the box upside down on the floor. There were vertical twigs in the door and windows. 'It's a jail.'

She started, glanced at the boy's mother. With her neck held stiff, the woman had been looking at her son's creation from the corner of her eyes. She looked morose, resigned.

'Is it for the men who did this to you?' the pharmacist asked.

The boy just adjusted the twigs.

'Bad people never end up happy,' she said. 'Sooner or later, they're punished. I believe that.'

'It's not for them.'

'For whom, then?'

'It's for us.'

The boy had turned the box, placed it so that its door was facing the entrance of the clinic and its sides were parallel to the walls of the corridor. The pharmacist, despite herself, reached out to touch the boy, but then, remembering how he'd shrugged her off earlier, pulled her fingers back.

His mother held her hand out towards him. 'Come.'

The boy walked on his knees to her, leaned against her leg with his cheek pressed to the side of her thigh. She passed her fingers through his hair, tucked a few strands behind his ears. The pharmacist saw the woman's eyes go once again to the clock, the hands of which were moving so slowly that she wondered if the presence of the dead had somehow drained its batteries.

The door of the operating room creaked open, and the teacher stepped out. Physically he didn't look any different from when he'd entered, except for the glass jar in his hand and the tube sticking out from under his shirt. But his face appeared wooden. The boy ran to his father and pressed his face to his side. The man cupped his son's head, moved him away from the tube.

The boy touched the jar. 'What's that?'

'I need to talk to you,' the man said to his wife.

'The operation went well?' She pushed herself up with her hands while balancing her neck.

'Yes, everything's fine.'

'Then what is it?'

'I'll tell you.' He gestured to the back room.

The boy looked alarmed. 'What are you going to talk about? I want to come too.'

'We'll be back in a few minutes. Stay here.'

'But why? What is it? Why can't I come with you?'

'Aai and I have to talk about something. A few things. We'll be back soon.'

'You can stay with me,' said the pharmacist. 'I'll get you some glue and scissors. We can make a nice house out of this.'

'It's not a *house.*'

The boy stamped on the box, made a hole in it with his heel, flattened the walls. With a kick, he sent it flying out of the clinic.

His mother began to bend to his height, but then seemed to remember her tube. She held her son against her pregnant belly, scolded him in a voice that had nothing but love in it.

'What is this? Is this any way to behave in front of Saheb and this nice madam? She's just trying to help you. Why shout at her?'

The boy twisted his mother's gown in his fists. 'Why don't you tell me what's happening? Why does Baba want to talk to you? The two of you are always hiding something.'

'Why would we hide anything from you, my prince? There's nothing to hide. I'm sure it's just something ordinary, boring. Like when Baba used to read the newspaper and you just wanted to look at the pictures, remember? I'm sure Baba wants to talk to me about something like that, something that wouldn't be interesting to you.'

The pharmacist forced a smile as she brought the smashed box back into the corridor. 'We can still fix this.

We can make whatever you want – a jail, a police station, anything. I have a lot of boxes. Come, sit with me while your parents talk.'

The man and his wife left the boy with the pharmacist. She did all she could to get his attention, but he kept turning to the door they'd closed behind them.

Saheb was trying to sit on the bench, wincing as he did so. The pharmacist knew how bad his back could get, with the slipped disc or whatever he had. It took him some time to settle there and release the arm with which he was propping his weight up on the bench. Then he raised his finger and held the tip close to his face. A small red drop squeezed out of it. The wood of the bench had splinters, she'd been pricked enough times herself. But Saheb just kept looking at the growing drop with a strange expression. 'I'll get some tape,' she said, and he, as if startled, shook his head and rubbed the drop off between his thumb and fingers.

She found the scissors, glue and some coloured paper in the pharmacy, laid the pieces of the boy's jail out on the floor of the corridor, and glued the sides back together. Once that was done, she started cutting another cardboard box into long strips to make a fence. The boy showed no interest in any of this.

'They're discussing the possibility of another surgery.'

It took a few moments for the boy to realize that Saheb was talking to him.

'Another surgery? When?'

'Now, before the sun rises.'

'Why?'

The pharmacist stopped her scissors midway through the cardboard. Saheb was speaking to the boy as if to an adult. Actually with more patience than he'd ever shown any adult. The boy listened without interrupting. When Saheb was done, the boy had questions, some of which Saheb answered. She'd never heard him say 'I don't know' so many times before.

Then the door of the back room opened, and the teacher and his wife returned to the corridor. The man nodded. 'Doctor Saheb.'

Saheb closed his eyes, stood up, stretched his back. 'We'll be back soon,' he said to the boy. 'You'll stay with her, won't you?'

The pharmacist smiled and widened her eyes at the boy despite the ache in her chest. The boy did not argue, just stayed with his head lowered. His mother remained where she was, looking away, her eyes still dry, very dry.

~

The surgeon entered the operating room once again, this time with the teacher and his wife in tow. He felt crippled with fatigue. The woman held his hand as she climbed up on the operating table.

'Have you felt your baby move inside you since that evening?' he asked.

'No. I remember feeling it kick at the village fair, a few hours before we were attacked.'

'So nothing in the afterlife? And how about tonight?'

'Nothing.'

'Did your official say anything about this?' he asked the teacher.

'No. I—I have to admit it didn't strike me to ask. I assumed that when he gave her life, he would also give it to the baby inside her. Don't they have the same life, the same blood, until someone cuts the cord?'

'That would be too simple, wouldn't it?' The surgeon placed his stethoscope against the woman's abdomen and listened at a few spots. 'I don't hear a heartbeat,' he said, and then, seeing their expressions change, added, 'but I wasn't really expecting the foetus to have one. I did, however, expect it to move and kick, just as you can.'

'What does this mean, Saheb?'

The surgeon lifted his glasses off his nose and tried to pinch with his thumb and middle finger the throbbing pain between his temples. 'I don't know. I *can't* know. Whatever I've learnt, all these decades of cutting people open and stitching them back together, nothing in them can help me answer your question. At this point, any guesses you can make will probably be more valid than mine.'

The teacher looked ready to crumble. His wife clutched her womb with a desperate look, as though through that grasp she could awaken the creature that might just be slumbering endlessly within.

'You understand why I'm recommending this, don't you?'

They nodded.

'You understand that we don't know how things will go in the morning. If I have to do an emergency delivery then, it could be dangerous for both mother and child. It's better to do it now, in a controlled setting. You understand that, right?'

'Yes.' They looked defeated, more dead now, so close to the morning, than they'd looked all night.

The surgeon replaced his glasses on the bridge of his nose. 'Do you believe that the official who sent you here is wise?'

'Yes.'

'And do you believe that he's benevolent?'

The teacher glanced at his wife, blinked at the floor a few times. 'Yes.'

'Then have faith in his wisdom and benevolence. Trust that he took every life, even the smallest one, into account when he arranged to send you here. Let's go ahead with the plan, but I should warn you, the child might not show any signs of life right now. It may be difficult for you to bear, but you'll have no choice but to wait until dawn.'

The teacher helped undress his wife and laid her flat on the operating table, supporting her head so the tube in her throat wouldn't be disturbed. He sat on a stool while the surgeon examined her.

Long striae ran across her stretched skin, testifying to the months she had spent on earth carrying a creature that, one flesh with her while she lived, had perished with her final breath. It was the only member of the family to return from the afterlife without wounds to its own body. If granted life, it could well survive without any medications or surgeries. After all, its battles with death would be those of every ordinary infant that had ever left a womb.

The surgeon felt the woman's uterus. The head was in the expected position – pointed down towards the pelvis. In the left part of the uterus, he could feel small irregular lumps – the cluster of hands, feet, knees – and on the right, there was the neat, firm curve of the spine. Everything was in its proper place. He picked the razor and shaved away the upper part of the woman's pubic hair. He then prepared the skin and draped it, pressed a roll of cloth against either flank.

He tried to recall what little he could about caesarean sections. The principles were simple enough, but he hadn't actually performed one in decades. He started with a neat horizontal incision, about six inches long, low on the abdomen, and cut through the skin, the connective tissue, the fat. He then cut through the fascia covering the vertical muscle in the midline, and pulled the two strips of muscle away to either side. Another few nicks with his scalpel, and he could peel the bladder and the fold of abdominal lining away from the lower segment of the uterus.

'Put on a pair of gloves. And take that fresh drape in your hands. Careful not to touch anything else, it's all sterile.'

When the teacher was ready, the surgeon put his scalpel to the uterus. It sank into the spongy muscle without difficulty, leaving a clean, bloodless gash. He had now grown accustomed to the absence of flowing blood. What a mercy it was not to have to constantly swab and suction, not to have vessels to clamp at every turn.

The firm globe of the child's skull, covered with soft, wet hair, was under his fingertips. He stretched the edges of the incision in the uterus, just as in those old textbook illustrations. 'It's time,' he said, more to himself than to anyone else, and with his right hand he reached into the womb, grasped the globe, and pulled.

The head emerged in a gush of amniotic fluid, within which it had remained suspended even in this unearthly state. The woman on the table gave a cry, though it wasn't one of pain, her eyes told him that. He held the head in both hands and pulled with his fingers looped around the neck. Nothing budged. The baby appeared locked in that position. He pulled, first with a gentle tug and then harder, but his grip was weak, so very weak, and he was afraid of damaging the slender neck with the strain. But what if he wasn't able to get it out? What if it remained stuck there, and dawn jumped up behind him that very instant? Mother and child would both start screaming, one head above, another below – a two-headed howling monster washed with fountains of blood. His tired hands just kept slithering around, and he adjusted the grip of his fingers, crooked an elbow. 'Come on,' he said, 'come on, don't be so stubborn.' Just when he felt he couldn't summon any more strength, there was a sudden give, the shoulders slithered through the incision, and the rest of the foetus poured out in such a slippery rush that he almost stumbled back with it. The remainder of the fluid in which it had floated drenched the drapes, splashed on his gown, and the strong odour of the womb and its fluid filled the room. He clamped and cut the umbilical cord, from the ends of which, predictably, there dripped no blood.

The infant's skin had a bluish hue, but unlike its parents it had nothing to mark it as an unnatural visitor to this world. Its arms and legs tapered into slender fingers and toes, and its face was perfectly formed, carved by some skilled hand made masterful in its craft through countless iterations. But, as the surgeon had feared, the infant did not move. It lay in his hands, its limbs flaccid, its eyes and brow still, its mouth in an unmoving yawn, fluid pooled at the back of its throat that it made no attempt to cough out. On any other night, this could have meant only one thing, for the laws of the earth did not allow the dead to return to life. But this night was different, when death could perhaps be the precursor of life, the herald of breath and blood. Who could know for certain? Despite the resolve with which he had prepared himself for this moment, the surgeon's eyes welled up at the sight of this stillborn infant. Lacking any device with which to suction its throat, he held it upside down by its ankles and patted it until all that could drip out of its mouth had dripped out. After wiping it dry, he handed it over to its father.

The teacher received the limp body in the coarse green cloth draped over his cupped hands, and lowered it until it was level with his wife's head. 'It's a girl,' he said. Both of them seemed overcome, as though for them the very appearance of death were still as potent as death itself. Perhaps justifiably so, for now the surgeon knew that neither in the land of the living nor the dead were miracles ever guaranteed, and that, except in the rarest of cases, death did not display its colours without good reason. The dead held and kissed the blue infant and seemed to be praying, though whether to a wise and benevolent God or to His wise and benevolent official, there was no way to tell.

The surgeon himself couldn't recall the last time he'd prayed. It wasn't something one could summon up after a lifetime of disuse. So he just voiced under his breath a hope that the child be not dead but only unborn, and that at dawn its blood might flow again and its lungs draw in the morning air and it would let out its first cry. The teacher held his weightless infant in one hand, while with the other he caressed his wife's cheek, and who could say whether he ached more for one than for the other?

The surgeon turned his eyes from them and allowed them to pray and lament in peace. Returning to his surgical field, he stripped the bloodless placenta from the interior of the womb, and with careful sutures he restored everything he'd divided with his knife.

Thirteen

The surgeon returned to the corridor to find the pharmacist and her husband emptying five large bags and stacking their contents on a bench. The man had managed to bring everything – antibiotics, pain medications, sedatives, rolls of cotton and gauze, cases of gloves, syringes, needles, suturing thread, catheters, tubing for intravenous fluids, and more bags of saline than the surgeon had dared list.

'I brought the blood too, Saheb.' The pharmacist's husband opened the icebox, displayed six red packets glistening with frost.

The man's shirt was drenched. His hair, his face, were covered with dust. The pharmacist, with an embarrassed look, was trying to make him more presentable by wiping the sweat off his forehead with a handkerchief.

'I was afraid something had happened,' the surgeon said. 'I was beginning to wish I hadn't asked you to go.'

'No, no, Saheb. Look, I'm back in one piece. No trouble along the way. Oh, before I forget, here's the rest of your money.'

He dug in his pocket and held out some notes. He was much shorter than the surgeon, barely taller than his own wife. In that moment, he looked like a schoolboy returning small change.

'Keep it.'

The man looked at his palm. 'I can't accept this. You're very kind to us. Too kind.'

Too kind? The man had travelled to the city and back, on bicycle and by rail, at a time of night when the honest world slept and only people of ill repute roamed the streets. He had carried in his pocket a sum large enough to invite an ambush, and then lugged back these heavy supplies without a soul to help him. Now, bathed in sweat, he stood declining a reward. The surgeon felt words rise to his throat, but he couldn't force them out. Why was it so difficult for him to express true gratitude, to speak freely, perhaps even let his eyes water at this earnestness?

The money would have to suffice for now. With his left hand, he folded the man's fingers and pressed them back over the notes in his palm. His right hand he gently placed on the pharmacist's head. The young couple stood like newlyweds, heads bowed, solemn, as though before a priest sanctioning their union in a sacred place. The surgeon willed with every thread of his being that they be guarded from evil, that they be spared all torments, that they never have to know suffering. He granted them health, peace, prosperity. He knew he had no power over anything, but he still blessed them with all that was his to give, and all that wasn't.

'You must be tired. You should go home.'

'No, Saheb. It's almost morning,' said the pharmacist. 'We can stay awake for a few more hours.'

And indeed the night had almost passed. In the east there was a darkness that wasn't entirely dark. The first sparks of day were glowing against the night's edge. The birds had already awakened, and were twittering and cawing in the trees. Cowbells sounded in the village.

'I've made you some tea, Saheb. Extra strong.'

He tried to smile, but the weight of what was yet to come was too great.

'Pour me a cup. I'll drink it soon.'

The boy flung down his scissors and ran to his parents the moment they stepped out of the operating room. His mother was cradling a bundle in her arms. The boy peered into the small opening in the swaddling. She adjusted the drape and showed him the round face circled by green folds.

'This is your sister.'

The boy studied the still face for a long time, then darted out his finger and tapped the little nose. 'Why doesn't she move? Why doesn't she open her eyes?'

'She's sleeping.'

'When will she wake up?'

'Soon. She'll wake up soon.'

'What will we name her?'

The teacher and his wife looked at each other. The woman spoke a name. The boy whispered it to the baby. 'Wake up,' he said, 'wake up,' shaking it as though, now armed with a name, he might be able to cajole it to life. But the baby did not move. Its cheeks remained blue.

'Gentle, gentle.' His mother folded a corner of the drape over the infant.

'I think it's time,' said the surgeon.

In a sombre and wordless procession, they followed him into the back room. He flicked on a light and saw that an extra mattress and sheet had been laid out on the floor. There was also a sturdy box padded with cloth to look like a crib. He hadn't had to ask the pharmacist for any of this; she'd done it all on her own. The teacher and his wife each sat on a bed while the son lay on the mattress on the floor. The surgeon could see the exquisite care they now took of the bandages and tubes sticking from their bodies. Maybe they too could feel how close it was, the moment when every stitch would be tested. The pharmacist and her husband waited in the doorway, and that left the surgeon at the centre of the circle formed by them all.

'I'm doing something I've never done before. After all my years of preparing the living for their deaths, I now have the task of preparing the dead for life. Sunrise isn't far, and neither you nor I really know what will happen then. The angel promised you life and blood, and I don't have any reason to doubt him, but how much blood and how much life he will give you, I can't say. I only hope it'll be sufficient.

'For our part, we've done everything we could. But look at the cracks in the walls, look at the rusted bed frames. Look at where you are. You can't leave this village, so your fates are tied to this clinic. I'll do everything I can, but there's no other doctor to relieve me. And I'm not a young man. I will stay awake as long as my body allows, but at some point I'll have to stop and rest.

'I'm not saying any of this to worry you. I'm saying this so that the three of you – yes, even you, my boy – should fully understand, or at least take some time to think about, the obstacles in front of us. If dawn brings life, it will also bring everything that comes with it – pain and infection and suffering. Your wounds will try to bleed, and though I've stitched them up as well as I could, I can't promise you that every knot I've tied will hold.

'Place the baby in the crib, lie down flat on your backs, and don't try to get up. I can't afford to have you faint and fall and suffer new injuries. As soon as your blood starts flowing, I will insert cannulas into your veins, and we'll give you fluids and antibiotics. Thanks to this man – he travelled all night for you – we now have some medications to help control your pain, and sedatives to make you drowsy if needed. But beyond that I don't have much more to offer. I don't have the skills or supplies to make you unconscious. Some of you might find that you have trouble breathing. I have two oxygen tanks here, both half full, but no life-support machines to stabilize you if things get really bad. So I must ask you to endure what is beyond my ability to control. And finally, I know you're very aware of it, but I'm still going to remind you: I *don't* have any skills beyond those of a simple doctor. If your lives slip from my hands, they're gone. I won't be able to reach into the other world and pull you back.

'I've done everything I could. I just hope it will help you face what is to come.'

He had closed his eyes while he spoke these last words, and when he finished, he found the teacher kneeling on the floor, shaking.

'Doctor Saheb, you have shown us more mercy than I ever hoped I would find. You, all of you, you are our saviours. As long as we live, and even beyond that, we will sing your praises to anyone who will listen. How can we repay your kindness, Saheb? I'll do whatever you want me to do, I'll work for you day and night, you won't need to pay me a single paisa. I'll help you care for your villagers. I hope they realize how blessed they are to have a saint like you among them. I know you don't like it when I say things like this, but that's what you are – a saint. More than a saint. And I can do nothing but fall at your feet.'

The man dived to the ground, and the surgeon jumped back. 'No, no, what is this? Don't do that.' He waved the teacher back to his bed. To avoid any further ceremony, he turned without meeting the eyes of the dead.

The pharmacist and her husband were at the door to the room. 'Keep a close watch,' he said to them. 'Call me if something happens.'

The cup of tea that the girl had poured for him was still steaming on the table of the consultation room. He picked it up and stepped outside the clinic. The glow in the east had deepened, but the sun had yet to cut through the horizon. He groaned at the stabs in his knees as he sat on the steps at the entrance.

At the bottom of the hillock, the village was like a primitive engine cranking its pieces into motion. Even if, by some miracle, the dead were able to keep from screaming in pain once they came to life, the usual villagers would soon start hobbling up to the clinic. He could make the pharmacist and her husband swear to secrecy – he trusted they would hold their tongues – but how long could he keep the visitors hidden? The villagers would have questions, perfectly valid ones. Where did these people come from? Why these injuries? Someone might call the district police. There would be an inquiry.

No matter how many explanations he turned over in his head, he couldn't cook up a single one that even the stupidest of constables would find convincing. Here was how the newspapers would report this: Three corpses had been found in a village clinic. A young family. The autopsies revealed gruesome findings. All of them had tubes in their flesh, and the boy's organs had been cut out. The woman's neck had been shredded and then stitched together with row after row of sutures. Her uterus had been sliced open, her dead foetus removed and placed in a crib next to her. There was no evidence that any anaesthesia was used. No trail of blood was found outside the clinic. No one had witnessed any struggle. The victims were clearly alive and intact when they reached this place. A crime of precise, horrific madness, planned and executed within the walls of this house of healing. A surgeon had become a butcher, brainwashed his superstitious assistants with tales of rebirth, and turned his clinic into a slaughterhouse.

He gulped short sips of tea. It was remarkable, the detachment with which he was able to think about this mess. It was almost as though he were contemplating the misfortunes of some poor fool who'd managed to lose himself in a deranged labyrinth. *Deranged* was really the only word for this. It was impossibly deranged, like some device of torture, full of traps and locks and monstrosities ... *dazzling*, now that he stopped to think about it. And it was exhausting, yes, dear god, all this thinking, it drained the life from every inch of his body, made his skin drape like a lead sheet over his bones.

He looked at his hands, so sore from the clamps and forceps and scalpels. There was life in them, precious little of it, but life nonetheless. The veil that separated the worlds of the living and the dead was now so thin that it might tear at the gentlest touch. Against this veil, he could feel his fingers pulse with a dull ache. And with blood – there was no separating the two, the blood and the ache, for, as he'd learnt from the dead, one couldn't exist without the other. His hands, unused for so long, whose inertia had caused him so much misery, had just completed a task that no surgeon would ever face, no matter how profound his skills or resources. Everything might well be uncertain, but his accomplishment was true, and would persist even when there was no one to recall it.

Grandiose thoughts, perhaps, but he allowed himself to think them. After all, the brightness in the east was growing every minute, and the world was preparing itself for something that had never before come to pass and never again would. If ever in all of history a moment deserved philosophical meanderings, it was this one.

'Whatever will happen will happen.'

With this thought he tried to rise, but the weight of the air pressed him back onto the stairs. The weight of his eyelids too, heavier than the earth itself. He allowed himself to shut them, just for a second, just to blink himself alert, and he felt the teacup slip from his fingers.

Before him grew a tree. It was a raw bud first, then a quick sapling in damp soil. Then an eruption filled the world, gnarled and mottled bark churned out of the earth, and leaves, like fluttering moths, fled from the trunk, drawing branches and twigs in their wake until the full, familiar form of the banyan stood under a cloudy sky. He recognized it – his old, estranged friend.

A boy was effortlessly climbing the tree. From his shoulder swung a bag, empty except for a few pages of newsprint. The branches left dry scratches on his arms. His slippers flapped, caught in the leaves, and he kicked them off. Beetles, crickets, caterpillars oozed from the bark, crawled along the endless branches. The tree was trying to bewilder him. It had built a maze to conceal the nest. It was clever, but not *that* clever, and he would outwit it.

For days, there were eggs in that nest, and by now they had to have hatched. The impatient skills of a surgeon squirmed in the boy's hands. The chicks would soon be his. He would first render them inert in formaldehyde, then stretch them out on a dissection board, pin their wings and limbs with needles. And then he would bare their lungs, their livers, their hearts, with his scalpel. He would sketch diagrams in his books, unearth organs that had never before been described. The new organs would be named after him. He would be listed in textbooks. Students would memorize his name for their exams. But the tree was jealous. It wouldn't share its bounty. It tried to confuse him with its green curtains. Once or twice he went down blind alleys, slipped and scrambled to regain his foothold. But he kept climbing.

And then suddenly there it was – the nest. He'd almost missed it in his hurry. The eggs had released their tenants into the world. The outsides of the shells were speckled with green, the insides white as ivory. The naked chicks thrashed. Twigs pricked their featherless sides, tried to warn them – they were no longer in their wombs; they should look around, beware. But they were still blind, their eyelids purple. The boy was out on the branch. It was flimsy but would support his weight. He extended his hand, cupping a piece of newspaper with which to scoop the chicks from the nest.

A crow flapped into view. It ignored him, brushed past his fingers, landed on the brim of the nest. At that sound, the nestlings balled themselves, opened their beaks, stretched their gullets. The boy pulled back his hand. The heavens opened, grub flowed from the mother's beak, and the nestlings fed. Their heads bobbed, their limbs scrabbled. And the boy allowed himself nothing more than the permission to perch on the branch and watch. Every nestling had something astonishing in it. Something that a single cut could destroy but not even a thousand stitches create.

But then the cloud that hung over the tree drifted away, dragging its shadow behind it. The lidless sun stared down. Walls of leaves keened in panic, darkened. Fire pruned them to meshes, revealed their hidden latticed veins. Spelled in them were the secret patterns of all life, glowing with a radiance he'd never known. The nest was just a ruse, a distraction the tree had used to draw his attention from the leaves themselves. He rushed to read them, to piece together this final mystery, but the sun burnt everything away.

Only nest and branch remained, jutting out of a naked tree. He was trapped. There was no foothold below him. No earth to which he could ever descend. The nestlings in their charring nest weakened, dried, thinned to skeletons, and their mother flew to battle the tyrant. With her sharp beak, she pecked at the sun, cracked open its shell, swallowed a drop of its molten yolk. The morsel scalded her throat, and her eyes bulged. Her wings convulsed like a cloak in a storm, an awful wound opened in her neck – a wound that no suture could ever close, and she uttered a caw.

But the caw was not the caw of a crow. It was the cry of a human. A cry of pain or surprise, maybe even the first cry of a newborn child. The tree, the nest, the crow, the nestlings, all turned to dust, and there it was again, the village laid out before him at the foot of the hill. And above it, the yellow edge of that ancient, deathless orb, creeping over the earth's rim.

Fourteen

It was like being slammed against a wall, this awakening. How much time had he been under? It couldn't have been long – the sun was below the horizon one instant and above it the next – but still he'd been dragged to such depths that he felt like a diver struggling to reach the surface. He lurched, hit his shin against a bench, felt the pain crackle in his bone, but still pushed on, feeling his way against the wall.

The corridor felt longer than he'd ever known it. The sounds continued, what seemed to be wailing, or screaming, yes, that was what it was, that high-pitched sound. Then someone called out to him, the pharmacist, perhaps. Her husband was clutching the doorframe, and she was hiding behind him. He turned the corner to the back room, and the instant he reached the doorway, everything fell absolutely silent.

He closed his eyes, dropped his head, shook it from side to side to throw off the shades that kept folding over his vision. The teacher was standing by the side of his bed.

There was dismay on the man's face, or something else, and his hand was held out in front of him, the wrist bent back and fingers fanned as if he were holding a blizzard at bay. The boy was on the mattress on the floor, propping himself up on a hand. When the surgeon looked at him, the boy started to lie down again, as though he'd suddenly remembered the instructions not to rise.

And then there was the woman. She was standing too. Her face was so different that the surgeon might not have recognized her were it not for the tube in her throat. It wasn't a grimace of pain, no, it was anger. Her lips were pulled back, her teeth pressed to each other. Was she the one who'd screamed? She was quiet now, though heaving with such emotion that he could hear her breath whistle through the tube.

But apart from this, none of the three looked any different. They weren't doubled over, weren't clutching their sides. They weren't fainting, falling. There were no rivers of blood. The baby in its crib was as limp as when he'd removed it from its womb.

The surgeon entered the room, and the teacher took a step back, raising his arm as though to shield himself. The surgeon grabbed the man's wrist. His own hand felt numb, as if someone had pumped it full of anaesthetic, but that was just the residue of sleep still coursing through his veins.

'Stop moving,' he said, and searched against the bones of the teacher's wrist. Once he'd found the spot, he held his fingers there.

There was no pulse.

He dropped the wrist, then pressed his fingers into the man's neck, poked under his jaw. Everything was still, lifeless. With the other hand the surgeon felt his own neck, and instantly his strong, fast pulse tapped back against his fingertips.

'How? It's already dawn. Then why hasn't—'

'Ask him, Doctor Saheb, *ask* him,' said the woman.

The pitch of her voice was so unlike the few meek sounds she'd made all night that he had to remind himself she was the same person.

Her husband cringed. 'Maybe it will take a little more time, Saheb. It should happen any moment now, and—'

'Don't *lie*,' said his wife, cutting him off in rage.

The boy jerked on the mattress at his mother's cry, drew his legs to his body, locked his arms around his knees.

'What ... what's this? What's going on?' the surgeon asked.

The teacher kept avoiding his eyes. The woman stabbed a finger at her husband. 'He just told me, Saheb. Right now, when I asked him why nothing was happening. Now, *now* he tells me, after everything—'

The man shrank under her. 'Saheb, forgive me, I really didn't think this would happen; so I didn't mention it to you.'

'Mention what?'

'The angel in the afterlife, he told me that things might not go exactly as planned. There could be a problem. He couldn't guarantee everything.'

'Problem? What are you saying? Tell me exactly what he told you.'

'The angel told us—'

'No,' his wife said. 'He told *you*. He didn't tell *me* anything. *You* alone.'

'The angel told me that the state in which we would be sent back, this state between life and death, he told me ... it wouldn't be easy to change us from this to living flesh. We have clots throughout our bodies – in every blood vessel, in the heart, in the brain. He would have to turn all of these to liquid and add new blood. Make it all flow. At the very same moment, he would have to bring every organ to life, all together, or we would immediately fall dead. He believed it could be done, but he'd never done it before. It was all very complicated. He tried to explain, but I didn't understand most of what he was saying. I just trusted him.'

'But you didn't trust *me*.' His wife was shrieking now. 'You didn't tell me.'

'If I'd told you, you would have refused. You wouldn't have come.'

'How dare you. That's my right. I had the right to refuse. It's my life. These are my children too. You told me everything would work out without any trouble.'

'That's not true. I never said that. I just ... I didn't want you to say no just because you were afraid.'

The surgeon put his hand out to shut them up. 'Now tell me again, slowly this time. What exactly did the angel say? What did he say would happen if your blood didn't start flowing at dawn?'

'He said that this, our return to life, it could be delayed.'

'How delayed?'

'He didn't say.'

'But still, did he mean hours? Days?'

'I don't know, Saheb. I just ... I don't know.'

'So it could be months. You could just remain stuck here like this.'

'No, I really ... I can't believe that the angel would let that happen.'

All the surgeon could do at this was shake his head. To have come all the way, *come back from the dead,* while leaving a question like this hanging. What could one even say about such folly?

'Did he at least tell you whether it would be the same for all of you? Or would this resurrection be more difficult for some than for others?'

Behind the teacher, the boy had been inching back along the floor. He was now cornered against the frame of his mother's bed.

The teacher pressed his eyes shut. 'The angel mentioned that some of us might come to life later than the others, and there was no way for him to know which would happen when. I assumed he meant the difference would be a few minutes. I didn't give it that much thought then, didn't ask him.'

An ear-splitting rasp jolted the surgeon. The woman had let herself sit down violently on the wire-frame bed, making the rusted legs scrape against the tiles. But no, nothing about her had changed. She just sat there with her palms pressed to the sides of her face, looking overwhelmed.

The surgeon's breath now drove through his nostrils in short, hot bursts. 'All night, every time you opened your mouth, you spoke about the dawn. Nothing else. Not a word about this.'

'I'm sorry, Doctor Saheb, I ... really, I'm sorry.'

'You didn't think I deserved to know any of this?'

'Saheb, I didn't want to complicate things. I hoped everything would go according to plan.'

'You decided to give me just enough information to keep me working, so that I would do whatever you needed.'

'No, Saheb, please don't say that. I trusted the angel. What else could I do?'

As abruptly as she'd dropped onto the bed, the woman now snapped to her feet and smoothed the gown that had bunched around her neck. Her face was stony. 'I'm going,' she said, a ghastly edge to her voice.

Her husband looked suffocated with fear. 'Where?'

'Back.' She reached into the crib, snatched up her infant. Its lifeless head rolled back, swaying against the side of her palm. She flung her other arm in her son's direction. 'Come.'

The boy cowered against the bed.

'Come,' she said again, but the boy just stared back, frozen on the floor.

She took two steps in his direction. The baby flopped in her hand. The pharmacist stepped from behind the surgeon, her hands held as though ready to catch the child if it should fall.

The woman now stretched her neck into forbidden angles as she bent down to grab her son. The boy's hands were bunched into fists. He dug them close to his body, hid them between his legs, behind his back. After trying a few times to find and grasp his fingers, she forced her hand into his armpit, tried to pull him up.

'Where are you going?' the surgeon asked.

'To the village boundary.'

The teacher now looked like a madman. 'No. No, you can't do that.'

'Why? That's better than this. Better than not knowing what will happen.'

'But then, then, why did we even come here?'

'Because you tricked us.' The woman's hair was smeared across her face. She tried to brush it away but couldn't, not with the infant in one arm and her son struggling in the other. 'Since the moment we reached the afterlife, returning here was all you could think of. I was trying to console myself, console us: now we're here, let's accept what we have, it's not as bad as you kept saying it was, let's take what God has given us and trust Him. But you? All you could think of was coming back to life. And for what? So that some of us could live and some of us die again? At least there we were all together.'

She dragged the boy to his feet.

'Baba, Baba.' He clutched at the frame of the bed.

'Stop this. Stop right now,' said the surgeon, but even his voice couldn't stay her. She tugged at her son until his fingers lost their grip on the metal rod. Her strength, her savagery, were astonishing. The surgeon tried to block her path.

'Please, just stop and think about this.'

'Saheb, I know what it's like to have my neck cut. To die. When he first started talking about this, this new life, I was so afraid of what we would have to go through. But I agreed, because I thought it would just be one night of waiting, and at the end of it we would endure whatever was in our fate. But now what's left? Just this fear. It's morning. Soon it will be afternoon, then night. And what are we supposed to do, Saheb? Wait for the pain? Lie down here until our bandages become wet with blood? No, I don't want to live like this. It won't be life. It will be worse than death. The afterlife might be bad, but not like this. I won't let my children suffer.'

The teacher forced himself past his wife. 'Please, just listen to me, I did what I thought was best. For us, for all of us.'

'Come with us if you want. All of us can go back.'

'You want to kill yourself? Kill our children?'

'Kill? How can I kill them? What's left in us to kill?'

The boy yanked his body back, snapped free of his mother's hold. She clawed at him, but her nails just scratched his skin as he fell back.

'Come, my baby, take my hand. Come with me.'

The boy crawled away from her on all fours, quailed in the corner of the room, his body pressed against the wall. He shook his head in terror.

'Please, just think a little,' the surgeon said to her. 'Think about what you're doing.'

The woman's face crumpled. With her fingers still splayed out, reaching across the room to her son, her eyes and lips twisted into a hideous, soundless wail.

The pharmacist tiptoed forward, slipped one hand under the infant's neglected head, the other under its buttocks, and the woman released it, slumped on the bed with her fingers like prison bars before her eyes, her nails digging into her scalp. The pharmacist's hands trembled as she replaced the corpse in its crib, and then, with a quiet motion, she slid the box along the floor and put some distance between mother and child.

It was a wonder the commotion hadn't yet brought every villager to the clinic. The surgeon looked around, but the corridor was empty except for the pharmacist's husband, who was standing outside the room with a look of bewilderment and fear. The portion of the hillock visible from the windows of the back room was fresh and serene in the morning.

The teacher returned to his bed and sat turned away from everyone, the weight of his body on an angled arm. He shielded his eyes with his free hand.

'Is there anything else?' the surgeon asked.

The man's hand remained where it was, concealing whatever shape guilt had given his features.

'Is there anything else you haven't told me?'

Through all this, the man had been protecting the jar connected to his chest. Air bubbled through it now with unseemly vigour.

'There's something more, isn't there? Put your hand on your son's head.'

'Saheb, please try to understand, please don't—'

The surgeon's eyelids were turning unbearably heavy again. Despite all this chaos, they kept dragging him down to some foggy abyss. There was a sickly shade to everything: the walls, the sunlight, the dead. They darkened, grew murkier, every time he blinked. He couldn't deal with these abominations any more. He just needed to fall on his own bed and lose consciousness.

'Swear on your son's head. Swear on the life you want him to have that there's nothing else I need to know.'

The teacher now turned like a criminal at an inquest. His face looked stretched across his cheekbones, his eyes seemed set deep under his eyebrows.

'Doctor Saheb, I should never have agreed, I should've said no when the angel told me.'

'Told you what?'

'I know now, I should have refused his offer there and then—'

'Stop talking in circles and get to the bloody point.'

The teacher's head sank into his shoulders. He raised his hands as if he were expecting his next words to be met with violence.

'The angel said that if something went really wrong, if there was a real risk that our secret might be exposed, he would have to pull us back to the afterlife. And with us, any living people who were involved in this.'

A high-pitched ring rose in the surgeon's ears over a painful silence, as if his hearing had, at that moment, been deadened by fireworks. He strained to make sense of the teacher's words, but no matter how hard he tried, he couldn't force them into a coherent sentence.

'What—'

'Saheb, I didn't think about how—'

'Any living person? But that means—'

'You are good people. I had no right—'

'You gambled with our *lives*. Without even knowing who we were.'

'No, Saheb, no, please, that's not how it happened. I was desperate. I was willing to do anything for my family. No one would ever have offered us anything like this again. I had to make a decision – it was then or never. I didn't think, I didn't consider how it would affect others, Saheb. I did an awful thing, but please don't blame my wife, my son. They didn't know any of this.'

'You ... you dared to talk to me about justice, about how unfair your deaths were—'

'I thought everything would go as planned, Saheb. I didn't expect any trouble. Even now, nothing bad has happened. We could come to life any minute, and then everything can just go on as it would.'

The man's naïveté was horrifying. The surgeon felt a cold thrust in his marrow, a pressure in all his bones, the greatest in his skull. Behind him, the pharmacist gasped. He heard it, but couldn't bring himself to look back at her. He curled his fingers around the free edge of the door panel to steady himself, but it swung and slammed against the wall with a loud thud, and he stumbled back with it. The teacher's body was convulsing, with sobs, it might be said, but the dryness of his eyes, the tearless contortions, they were all too macabre to have any real meaning. It was as though the night had started all over again: the dead had just appeared with their mad predicament, and he was at the mercy of it all.

'Call your angel.'

The man seemed not to hear him at first, and then his face flattened into a stare.

'He responds to your summons, right? Summon him now.'

'But, Saheb, that was in the afterlife. He can't come here.'

'You told me they could if they wanted to.'

'Doctor Saheb, please understand. The angel can't ... *won't* come to this village.'

'Then what are we supposed to do? None of you know what's going to happen. Only the angel knows.'

'But he won't—'

'You fucking fool, why are you wasting my time arguing? After everything you've done? Just summon him.'

The teacher seemed to wither under the surgeon's fury. He slowly rose from the bed, joined his shaking hands together, pressed them to his lips.

Then he shut his eyes and started muttering, reciting some prayer in a tongue that the surgeon couldn't recognize. It went on and on. The man didn't stop for breath – of course he had no need for it, he could very well continue this till the sun was doused and the moon ground back to dust. The surgeon felt a sudden, racking chill at the thought of a celestial being actually appearing in his clinic, glowing like a firefly. What would he do then? Plead for his life and the lives of the others, beg for pity from this being that probably considered him no more worthy of life than a cockroach?

But nothing changed. Even the air stayed completely still. The surgeon looked around, and saw that the boy was still in the corner of the room. He was hugging his knees to his face, his head bent so that his terrified eyes peered through the mess of hair on his brow. His mother's face was turned away towards the far wall, whether from anger or shame or grief, there was no way to tell. Or maybe because she couldn't bear to see this, the figure of her humiliated husband in his useless prayer. A miserable rhythm had entered the man's recitation by now, the same incoherent string of syllables rising and sinking from the waves.

The surgeon turned. The pharmacist pulled back behind her husband. Their faces were pale, and there was reproach in their eyes, or at least that's what he saw. *You dragged us into this, Saheb,* he heard, but neither of them had spoken. There was no assurance he could give them now; so he just looked past them and walked into the corridor.

A few syringes, still in their plastic packaging, were strewn across the floor. They'd probably spilled from their boxes when he hit his shin against the bench. At that memory, the pain returned, and he bent, felt the spot with his finger. His trouser leg was wet there. The spilling of morning blood by the wrong character in this farce. The omen of death. The wait couldn't be long now. A few hours at the most. What would it be like to die at the whim of a bureaucrat? A brisk, banal leaving from a body that would then fall and fracture itself, at which point who cared – once you're dead, you're dead, no matter what anyone promises you. But the girl and her husband, for it to happen to them ... No, it was too horrible even to consider. If there were to be deaths, he should die thrice, but not them, god, not them.

Tears formed under his eyelids, but he was tired, too tired, and they couldn't even wet his eyes, not even when he tried to massage them out with his palms. The muttering continued in the back room. It hadn't stopped even after he'd left their presence. It was idiotic, absurd beyond words, to expect an official of the afterlife to report to the insects of the earth. The entrance to the clinic was just a few feet away, so the surgeon stumbled to it. Who knew, perhaps the air there would be easier to pull into his lungs?

And that's when he saw. Some distance away, on the gravel path leading up to the clinic, the official. The one who had brought the polio vaccines the previous afternoon.

Fifteen

The surgeon felt his innards churn with a sickening rush. He tried to convince himself that he was mistaken, but there was no doubt about it. It was the same official. As far as he could tell, the man was even in the same blue safari jacket he'd worn the previous day.

The official looked back at him, and the surgeon passed his gaze over the horizon as though he were just examining the morning landscape. Then he turned as calmly as he possibly could and walked to the back room.

The pharmacist and her husband were squatting outside the door, huddled against each other. The teacher was still standing in closed-eyed recitation. The woman, the boy, the newborn – all were just as he had left them.

The surgeon had to force the words from his throat. 'All of you, listen very carefully. I won't repeat this. Lock yourself in and don't make a sound. And don't come out until I call you, no matter what happens.'

The teacher stopped his prayer, returned to the surgeon a look that was initially blank but then curdled with shock.

'How—,' he began, but nothing else emerged from his lips. His hands remained where they were, the fingertips touching in front of his chest. He was taking too long to collect his senses, and his wife rose from her bed, swung shut the leaves of the door, slid home the bolt.

The pharmacist began to pull her husband into the pharmacy.

'Not there,' said the surgeon, pointing out the open window in the front wall.

So the two stole to the other side of the corridor, past the autoclave machine, and into the operating room. The surgeon couldn't remember if he'd left the placenta lying on a tray there, but it was too late to worry about that now. The door closed behind the girl and her husband.

It would be better if he were seated when he faced the official, the surgeon decided. It would rid his legs of the obligation to be steady. On a whim he happened to glance at the autoclave, and saw the small red light glowing on its lid. At the very thought of its unpredictable shriek, he flipped off the wall switch and pulled out the plug.

A crunch sounded outside the clinic before he could reach the consultation room, and so he stayed in the corridor and turned to face the entrance. His fingers knotted behind his back, he straightened himself to his full height. Biting the back of his lower lip to still the quiver in his jaw, he tried to settle his forehead into some expression of bland and appropriate surprise. Before he could achieve any of this, the official appeared, framed in the doorway, the sky at his back.

'Good morning, Doctor Saheb. Hard at work, I can see.'

He climbed up the few steps at the door.

'Quite a strange decision. Whoever it was that drew out the plans for this clinic, why did they put it high up on a hillock like this? The sicker your patients are, the less likely they are to make it to this place. A clinic only for the healthy, eh?'

The official didn't appear winded by the climb. That said, he wasn't carrying any boxes today. He cast a look around the corridor, at the supplies piled on the benches, the packets on the floor.

Now the surgeon had to say something, play host on this morning that was proving more grotesque than the night that preceded it. He unlocked his fingers from behind himself and gestured to the consultation room.

'Would you like some tea? I had made a kettle for myself.'

The official showed no sign he'd noticed the tremor in the surgeon's voice. 'Yes, why not?'

The surgeon led the way into the room, his back as stiffly held as when he'd received the official. The pharmacist had left the kettle on the side table as always. He poured a cup.

'You look tired, Saheb.'

The surgeon hadn't glanced into a mirror since the previous morning, but he could imagine how darkly the night had shaded the folds around his eyes.

'I have to say,' the official said, 'this is quite a change from the welcome you gave me yesterday.'

The surgeon placed the cup on the official's side of the table. The tea was lukewarm – no steam curling up from the surface. His own teacup, he now remembered, was somewhere on the gravel outside the clinic entrance. His chair gave its familiar creak under his weight, and his fingertips left moist oval smudges on the plate of glass on his desk. There were things flattened under it – yellowed receipts, scraps with faded scribbles, flowers with their anthers spread out.

'How did the drive go, Saheb?'

'The drive?'

'The vaccines. Did you end up using them all?'

'Yes, all.'

'Good, that's good. It's to be admired, what you do here, and with so little.'

'I try.'

'There aren't too many surgeons working in broken-down clinics like this.'

'Hmm.'

'It must be difficult, working in this place.'

'Difficult, yes.'

'Especially with you having to spend from your pocket to stock the pharmacy.'

'Yes.'

'Unfortunate that you have to balance your needs against those of the clinic.'

'I do what I can.'

The official had settled in his chair, his soft, full hands folded on his belly. His nails were small and circular, with neat crescent edges. A second chin occasionally formed under his face when he spoke. He hadn't touched his tea.

'You've heard the story of the Brahmin and the Ganga, haven't you, Doctor Saheb?'

'Uh...'

'I'm sure you have. Maybe you've forgotten it. In any case, here it is. There once was a poor Brahmin who lived all alone. As the years went by, his spine bent from age, his hair turned white, and the time came when he knew he would die. Now he had only one wish: to bathe in the water of the Ganga before he closed his eyes for the last time.

'But our Brahmin had never left his little village. What did *he* know about the world? Someone told him that the Ganga was to the north. So this poor man sold all his belongings, settled his debts, and set off with a stick and a bundle of food.

'After half a day's walk, he reached a small stream. He put down his bundle, dipped his hands in the water, and started to pour it over his head.

'A farmer from his village happened to be walking to the market. He recognized the Brahmin and asked, "Washing your clothes?"

'"No, I'm cleansing myself," replied the Brahmin. "This water from Gangotri, it will wash my sins away. Then I can die in peace."

'"But this isn't the Ganga," the farmer said. "This is just a little stream. The Ganga is much farther away."

'So the Brahmin, weak as he was, gathered up his things and hobbled along. The hot ground burned his feet. For every hour he walked, he had to rest for two more.

'Two days went by, and he came to a river. He said his prayers, bowed to God, and entered the water. A shepherd on the riverbank asked, "Why are you praying here, grandfather?"

'"My son, I'm washing my sins away," said the Brahmin. "I'm preparing myself for death."

'"Washing sins? In *this* water? This is just a small river, grandfather. It feeds our fields, nothing more. If you're looking for the Ganga, you should keep walking."

'The Brahmin had so little strength left, but what else could he do? He begged along the way for food to keep his soul tied to his body. He had to stop and rest his bones every few minutes now – under trees, under large rocks, any place he could find.

'A few days later, he reached another river – a wide and mighty one. He waded into it with tears flowing down his cheeks. So great was his joy that all the pain racking his body seemed to vanish. With all his faith and devotion, he said his final prayers, bathed in the water, and purified himself.

'A fisherman passing in his canoe cried out, "Watch out, old man. You'll drown if you aren't careful."

'The Brahmin smiled. "We all have to die someday. Me much sooner than you. Drowning in the Ganga would be a blessing. It would take me straight to heaven."

'The fisherman laughed so hard that his canoe almost tipped over. "The *Ganga*? You toothless fool. Who told you this was the Ganga? This river is nothing, just a tributary. Go, cross the bridge and keep walking northwards."

'By now, the Brahmin had become so ill that he could hardly breathe. Every step he took made him feel lightheaded. His skin burned with fever, no food or water would go down his throat. He knew death wasn't far.

'A crowd of people joined the road. They were dressed well, all in a festive mood. "Why are you so happy?" the Brahmin asked a boy in the group.

'"Because we're all going for a dip in the Ganga," the boy said. "It's very close now."

'The old Brahmin was filled with despair, because he knew it was too late. He swung forward on his stick, as fast as he could go, and tried to keep up with the other travellers, but they passed him one by one. His legs became heavy as grindstones. The Ganga, the real one this time, blue and immense, stretched out at the horizon. But the fever had spread through his whole body, and there was a crushing pain in his chest. His stick slipped from his hand, and he fell on the mud, dead.

'His soul left his body and reached the other world. He stood in front of Chitragupta, who was there with his book of sins and virtues.

'The Brahmin cried, "O great Lord, I couldn't cleanse myself. I'm full of sin. Send me to the underworld if you wish, for I was unable to bathe in the Ganga."

'All Chitragupta said was, "Ah, my son, but you're mistaken," and he opened the door to welcome the Brahmin into heaven.

'That's the story, Doctor Saheb. Quite a touching one, wouldn't you agree? Now tell me, what would you say is the moral of this tale?'

On any ordinary day, the hectoring tone of this fable would have enraged the surgeon. Even now, he could barely believe he'd just allowed himself to sit there and be spoken to for so long in such a condescending tone. But when he tried to reply, he found he could only mumble.

'The moral? Even a stream can ... can be as holy as the Ganga if ... if you have faith. Is that what you want me to say?'

The official raised his forefinger with a lecturer's air. 'That's what everyone thinks. You're not the only one to come up with this optimistic interpretation. But let me suggest something else. I've thought about this tale a lot, and I've realized that the true moral is actually quite different. It's that there is no Ganga.'

'No Ganga?'

'Well, of course there's the river that starts at Gangotri, joins the Yamuna, empties into the ocean, all of that. But the Ganga that the Brahmin was looking for, the one that can wash away sins – it simply doesn't exist. There's nothing in its waters that gives it any magical powers. You know that, Saheb, as well as I do.'

'So that's the moral? That there's no way to wash away your sins?'

'Not exactly. It's that everything about sin lies in how you choose to look at it. The Brahmin chose to believe he was washing his sins away, even though it was in a minor river. It was a compromise, but it was the best he could do, and, as it turned out, it was good enough for Chitragupta. That's what we're all limited to, you and I – compromises.

There is no Ganga. You just pick a river and decide that its water is holy. And then it's better if you don't look back.'

This new blend of delirium and fear the surgeon felt made even the terrors of the previous night seem mundane. Perhaps this was why the heads of the condemned were covered with sacks, so that they might be spared the horror of a final conversation with the executioner while the noose was being adjusted.

'Tell me, Saheb, what river have you chosen in life?'

'I just ... I try my best to help. Help those who come to me.'

'And what do you expect out of it? For yourself?'

'Nothing much any more. Only that I be allowed to live my life. That the people who work for me not be harmed.'

'That's it? A balance of lives? That's how you think about it?'

'I try not to, but there are times.'

'And tell me, if you find yourself in a position where you have to harm someone to preserve your own life, what would you do?'

'Choose the just path. I hope I would have the courage.'

'And what would the just path be?'

'It would depend on the circumstance.'

'A different river each time?'

'If you insist on that word, then yes.'

'And how would you choose between them?'

'As you said just a minute ago, you just pick one and decide that its water is holy.'

The surgeon said this in as a grim a tone as possible, but somehow it still amused the official enough to make him slap his hand on his thigh. 'Very clever, Doctor Saheb. My own words turned back against me. Very clever.'

The suffocating coils of sleep, even at a time like this, draped around the surgeon's muscles, folded over his brain. Whatever was to happen, no matter how terrible, he hoped it would happen soon. But the official showed no sign that he wanted to stop speaking.

'Tell me, Saheb, do you believe in God?'

'Me? No. I've ... I've never been God-fearing.'

'God-fearing ... Hmm. People use the term all the time, but it's a strange one if you stop to think about it. Especially since God is supposed to be everywhere – in the earth, in the sky. But people don't spend their lives fearing the earth and sky.'

'Maybe they should.'

'But you see, when the earth or sky kills you, it does so indiscriminately, without making any plans. God, on the other hand, He has a mind, He thinks. That's what makes Him worthy of fear. Because no one knows what He's planning. So you play games with Him, try to understand His mind.'

'Play a game with God? How do you do that?'

'Well, you can't. If you set up a chessboard on the street and challenge God, He won't come down to move His pieces. But a passer-by might. That's how the game begins. And the passer-by is already playing other games. He's quarrelling with his brother over their father's will, extracting a loan from a bank, looking to fondle some woman's breasts without having to hang a mangalsutra between them. Each game is small, but they're all pieces of larger games, and the largest one, the one that contains them all, that's the game you play with God.'

His life and the lives of everyone else in the clinic, were in the hands of this unhinged official. And it wasn't just drowsiness he was feeling. It was a slippage into non-existence – the world and everything in it scattering to pieces that no one, not even God, could ever put back together. The official kept talking about the stupidity of the pious: 'holy threads around their bodies, eating certain foods on certain days, smearing ash on their foreheads', about how God despised worship: 'The villagers who fawn over you, Doctor Saheb, do you feel anything for them but contempt?', about the mind of God: 'He places puzzles in the world so that He can understand it better'. The surgeon had been under anaesthesia only once in his life, when his gall bladder was removed. What he was feeling now was no different from how he'd felt in the moments after propofol was injected into his vein. He selected a red spot on a scrap of paper on the desk, tried to keep its redness burning into his retina. The world couldn't dissolve, he declared, as long as he kept this redness from leaching out. A single mind, if it wanted, could hold all of existence to ransom with a single red spot.

'...All you can do is play His games. That's why God keeps the universe going: to see what new moves he can learn from His creatures.' The official adjusted himself in his chair. A smile spread under his moustache. 'And death, that's the most ingenious of all His games. You've made your share of moves in that one, haven't you, Saheb?'

A bead of sweat cut a slow path down the side of the surgeon's face. When he saw the official's eyes follow it from brow to cheek, he wiped it away with a quick brush of his palm. On the official's face itself, there wasn't a trace of moisture. And his skin was smooth, incredibly smooth.

'You haven't had your tea. Please. It must be growing cold.'

'I will, I will,' said the official, without making any effort to reach for the cup. His moustache, his hair, were a deep, unnatural black.

'And what is this? Is this a game as well?'

'This, Saheb? You mean my visit?'

'Yes. Why are you here?'

'I have as much of a right to be here as you. Tell me, why did you decide to become a surgeon?'

'I ... I don't even know any more.'

'Still, why?'

'It seemed, during my training, that holding a diseased organ in my hand and cutting it out, it was a straightforward way of doing things.'

'That makes sense, yes. And tell me, what gives you greater satisfaction, cutting people open or stitching them back?'

'What?'

'Of all the creatures on earth, only humans can put things back together. But the ability to tear flesh apart –

God gave it to every beast roaming in the jungle. So there must be something to it, some animal pleasure. Like eating and drinking. Or sex. It must fulfil some basic need.'

'What a *horrible*—'

'I'm just asking. You have skills that I don't. So I can only learn these things through you. I like to ask questions, understand new things. Tell me, when you cut someone open, do you feel a thrill?'

'Stop, that's just, you can't—'

'To lower your hands into someone's body and know that you hold their lives in the snip of a scissor, it must give you such a sense of power.'

'No, no—'

'What do you feel during a surgery, then? Answer me.'

'Fear, it's fear. Above everything else.'

'Ah. Fear of what?'

'What do you want?'

'You can't just have fear. It has to be fear of something.'

'What do you want from me?'

'Your surgical skills, are you satisfied with what they've brought you?'

The surgeon's lips, his tongue, scratched against each other now, rough as sandpaper. The official leaned forward.

'Whatever you're feeling, Saheb, it's quite understandable. It can't be an easy thing, accepting that someone you treated like a rat yesterday has more power over you today than you could have imagined.'

The official now picked up the cup. The tea was clearly cold by now, but he still blew on its surface before taking a sip. 'You see, after our little meeting yesterday, I went straight to the head office to take a look at your file. You were such an unusual character, I had to learn your story, find out how someone like you ended up here. There are rooms upon rooms there, you can imagine, cabinets to the ceiling. It took me all evening, but I found it just as I was ready to give up.'

The surgeon's nerves, the strands of his hair, all stabbed like copper barbs. His eyes felt intensely clear.

'You know a lot about compromise, don't you, Saheb? People like you, you stand over others and lecture them about integrity, and then when it's time to save your own skin, you soil your hands in the same dung. Your file is quite thick, I'm sure you know. Newspaper clippings, court records, all those things.

'At one level, I don't blame you. Look, mistakes happen. If I were in your place, I would have tried to bribe that other surgeon as well. When a patient is dead, he's dead, it's bad enough. Why rake up trouble for the doctor on top of that? But you never know what the person on the other side will be like. Unlucky for you that your opponent ended up being a disciple of Gandhi.'

The surgeon studied the flowers flattened under the glass, their dry, brown, dead petals.

'All these supplies in the corridor, Saheb, they weren't here yesterday when I checked. You'd hidden them somewhere. Just like you're hiding that dealer in the back room right now. Look, I'm an understanding man. I know they don't pay you enough. Selling supplies under the table, everyone does it – you're not the only one, I'm not judging you. But they don't pay me enough either. Not enough for me to keep my mouth shut when I see something like this.'

A slow, heavy drip gathered in the surgeon's gullet, swelled painfully behind his breastbone. The official finished his tea, wiped off a few drops hanging from his moustache, and sat straight in his chair. His fleshy face beamed.

'It's all up to you. If you think I'm just bluffing, then fine, I'll make some calls, and my colleagues and I, we'll make a detailed search and inventory of the clinic, go through all past records, interview the villagers about suspicious activity, all the routine stuff. I'm a decent man. I can keep my mouth shut. But I can't promise you that the other officials won't let something slip to the villagers about your past.'

The surgeon reached into his back pocket. 'Here.'

The official looked at the two notes the surgeon had held out. 'I have a wife and children, Saheb. My daughters are yet to be married. Whatever we think of this world, we still have to live in it.'

The surgeon blinked at the money, then stuffed the notes back into his wallet. As he rose from his chair, a sharp pain pulled at his spine, and he stayed that way for a few seconds, stuck in that awkward pose. Then he limped to the safe and turned the lock. There was just one bundle in it, and a few scattered notes. He pulled out the bundle.

There was no way for the surgeon to know if he'd overshot the usual amount for this sort of bribe. The official probably had enough practice with such dealings that he could keep his eyelids steady in a sandstorm. He took the bundle and started counting through it with the elegance of a bank teller.

'Promise me I won't see your face again,' said the surgeon.

A softness entered the official's manner, ripened with his progress through the bundle. 'I wish I could promise you that, Saheb, but I've been assigned to this clinic. Unless they replace me, it's my job to check in once in a while. From your point of view, it's good it's me and not someone else, because who knows what my replacement might be like? But let me promise you this: you won't see me for many months, let's say six. I won't stop by, I won't let any other official bother you, and what's more, I'll make sure all of your supplies are delivered without a hitch. Then you can do whatever you want with them, and put down in your account books whatever you like. I'll just rubber-stamp them.'

Now done with his counting, the official folded the notes into a pocket in the lining of his trouser waist. He joined his palms to each other and made an exaggerated bow. And then he left. Feeling his eyelashes dampen, the surgeon turned to the wall.

'I almost forgot, Saheb.'

The official was in the doorway again, pointing at the polio vaccine ledger that lay shut at the edge of the desk.

The same ledger whose columns the surgeon had been filling with numbers and calculations before the dead first appeared. That was why the official had returned to the clinic this morning: to collect the ledger and file it away in the head office. The man stood there as though expecting the book to be handed to him, but after a few moments passed in silence, he stepped in, picked it up without bothering to check its pages, and stepped over the blister-packed syringes in the corridor on his way out.

Sixteen

The haze of morning seemed to give even the peeling paint a surreal air, making it appear as though the clinic were casting off its old skin in an attempt at rebirth. A particularly large flake hung from the ceiling of the consultation room like an icicle. The surgeon let his eyes rest on it between glances at the window. Watching the official's diminishing form was like staring into the sun – he could only endure a few moments of it before he had to turn his eyes away. There was a final insult in the man's indifferent gait, in the way he strode without looking back, without a shred of further curiosity about the clinic or its contents. At the base of the hillock, the road curved, and the official disappeared behind a crumbling wall.

'He's gone,' the surgeon called out. A weariness of death and of everything on either side of it filled him.

The operating room was the first to open, and the pharmacist appeared at his door. 'What did he want, Saheb?'

'Nothing. Some paperwork.'

The way the pharmacist was staring at him, the expression on her face, it made the surgeon wonder if he too had joined the ranks of the dead. Under the table, he placed the fingers of one hand on the wrist of the other. He still had a pulse.

Then the door to the back room opened. The teacher approached with a shuffling walk. He seemed to be in great pain, though not from his wounds. Nothing had changed there.

'Doctor Saheb, I don't know how to ... I don't have any words, but please forgive me, please understand why—'

The teacher's jaw moved as he spoke, as did the flesh and skin of his face, all dead, of course, but imitating life with a terrible talent that the surgeon knew he would never understand as long as he lived. No amount of pondering would help, nor rummaging through ribs or guts. Perhaps that was why one died: so that one could finally fathom death.

'Close the door,' the surgeon said.

The pharmacist and her husband remained in the corridor as the teacher pushed the door shut after him. The man sank to his knees, and the jar attached to the tube in his chest clattered to a halt beside him. He seemed to be searching the surgeon's eyes for compassion, but the surgeon wasn't sure he had any left.

'The official you told me about while I was operating on you – not the one who sent you here, the other one, the one who was punished because he gave all those unnatural powers to humans – were you telling the truth about him?'

'Yes, Saheb, all true. I told you exactly what he said to me.'

'Now think very carefully, and answer me only after you've taken the time to do so. Is there any possibility that you lied to me about this other official? Is there any possibility that the official who sent you here and the official who was toying with humans, they were one and the same, and you just cooked up a new character to conceal that part of his past?'

'I swear, I promise you, they were different. Completely different.'

It was a pity, thought the surgeon, that he would never be able to trust the teacher again, no matter how much sincerity the man put into his words.

'And the official who sent you here, is it possible that he's toying with you, and with me? That we're all puppets, and he's just entertaining himself?'

The man didn't blurt out an answer this time. This question was clearly not entirely foreign to his thoughts.

'When the official offered to help us, I have to admit that my first fear was that this was some kind of trap. But why would he play with us like this? What could he gain from it?'

'Does a puppeteer need a purpose?'

'With lives, Saheb? How cruel would he have to be?'

'Have you ever seen a cockfight? There was one in this village a few months ago. They attached knives to the roosters' feet.'

'The official wouldn't do that to us, I'm telling you. He isn't that kind of person.'

'He *isn't* a person.'

The surgeon reached for the cup from which the earthly official had drunk. It was empty except for a sediment of tea powder at its bottom. One could read the future in it, or so he'd heard. He rolled the cup in his fingers, wondering whose future it was supposed to be – his or the official's.

'I don't know what's worse,' he said. 'A bureaucracy that forces you to bribe, or one in which bribery isn't even an option.'

'Saheb, there's at least one official in the afterlife who's willing to break unjust rules. Someone who is kind. Maybe there are more.'

'Yes, and look at what his kindness has brought you.'

'It's helped us meet you, Saheb. Even if we die again this very moment, we would still be blessed by the hours we've spent in the presence of a great man.'

The obsequious way the teacher kept twisting his fingers into coils aggravated the surgeon. He walked the teacup to the side table. If he were to smash it, it would just create shards for the pharmacist to sweep up. It was a sign of cowardice anyway, the venting of anger on inanimate things. The surgeon let the cup clatter onto the tray.

'When you speak this kind of nonsense,' he spat, 'it just makes me wonder if you have more lies to reveal, if you're fattening me with flattery before you betray me again.'

The teacher recoiled at these words. His pathetic expression infuriated the surgeon further.

'Maybe I should just announce this in the village square? "Gather around, O villagers, and listen to me. The dead are here to live, or rather, remain dead, among us. Let's welcome them into our community."'

'I really, Saheb ... I don't know if it's a good idea to even think about something like that. The official might be forced to kill everyone—'

'How the fuck does it matter? We're slaves in both worlds either way. And your official wouldn't dare kill a whole village, would he? Maybe that's what I should do: announce this to the villagers right away, and then the officials, for once, won't have a choice—'

'Please, Saheb, please don't say that. The official is listening to everything, I'm sure—'

The surgeon was in a state beyond sleep now. It was a dense, saturating daze from which there could be no sleeping or awakening. He collapsed back into his chair.

'What the *hell* am I supposed to do with you people then?'

The teacher looked shattered. 'My wife was right. We should never have come.'

'Yes, you shouldn't have. You should have stayed where you were.'

'We'll go, Saheb. We don't want to make any more trouble for you.'

The surgeon slammed his hands on the desk and planted his brow on the backs of his knuckles. He blew his breath out against the glass in frustration.

'Yes, keep coming up with more ridiculous ideas like that. Even if you make it to the village boundary without being seen, you'll still leave your bodies behind. With the surgeries you've had, no matter what happens, everything will be traced back to me. And *I'll* be the one who'll die in prison.'

There was a long silence. And then the teacher spoke, his words so muted that the surgeon had to strain to hear them.

'We could ... Saheb, if you know of any abandoned well, somewhere outside the village ... Or I could help you dig a hole at night. Like a grave...'

The surgeon did not lift his face from the glass. And he did not reply. To his shock, his tongue did not lash out to reject the offer the moment it was spoken. Yes, he knew of a spot near the southern edge of the village, behind a decrepit temple that no one visited because the idol in it was said to be cursed. And yes, there was a secluded path to it from the clinic, down the side of the hillock farthest from the farms and huts.

He couldn't involve the pharmacist and her husband in this, of course. They'd done so much, and might be willing to do more, but he couldn't ask *this* of them. This would have to be his doing and his alone. After midnight, he would have to tiptoe with the dead to the thicket behind the temple. If they were careful, they could manage the journey without being seen. Yes, graves would have to be dug. Deep ones, capable of guarding their secrets. The teacher would have to do most of the digging – he was the younger, stronger man. He would have to ready the earth for the task of swallowing his family.

And then the surgeon would lead the dead to the village boundary. There they would drop. Return to their true forms. Become corpses like any other. Then they would have to be dragged. Pushed into graves. Soil would have to be shovelled over them.

The hypnotic horror of this contemplation was unfolding in the face of the surgeon's efforts to stop it. With the force of a hurricane, it was ripping through every vestige of sanity and decency in his brain. Ever since the dead had appeared in his clinic, he'd spent every minute in detailed planning. Every cut, every stitch, every surgical instrument – he had outlined and rationed them all. How was he supposed to switch off this faculty? Especially now, at the end of all things?

And indeed a logistical problem was already presenting itself: Where exactly *was* the boundary of the village? There were stone markers at a few spots where one village ended and another began, but what was the precise location at which the dead would turn inanimate? Did the boundaries marked by the government correspond exactly to those respected by the afterlife? This question had to be answered before the graves could be dug. Otherwise, who knew what distance he'd have to drag their bodies?

It meant that one of the dead would have to walk ahead of the others. Like a canary meant to be snuffed. A mother couldn't be expected to endure the demise of her son. And a boy couldn't be asked to witness it of his parents. The man couldn't be the first to go, for he had to remain capable of digging. The best option was for mother and son to walk together. She would want to carry her infant.

Step after step they would advance, the moon lighting their path. Ten paces behind them would follow the teacher. And the surgeon would trail them all, so that he wouldn't have to look upon the face of the father at the moment when his beloved ones crumpled to the ground.

The surgeon sat up with a jerk. The teacher, still kneeling on the floor before him, started at the movement. On the man's face was a gathering horror. The surgeon couldn't quite tell if the teacher had been serious when he'd offered his suggestion, but it was clear that he could see now that it was the only way forward. Perhaps he too understood what would be required of him.

And the surgeon saw in that instant the depths of his own degradation. How completely his soul had been eroded, how the years had torn the stuffings out of his humanity and left him hollow. He should never have become a surgeon. He should have remained a coroner. His place had always been with the dead who remained dead. Those who lay on slabs and did not speak. Who asked nothing of him and to whom he owed nothing.

A voice called from the corridor. 'S—Saheb, Saheb.'

It was the pharmacist. Neither the surgeon nor the teacher moved. There was a sound of knuckles rapping against wood, but neither of them responded. The rapping grew louder, more urgent. The surgeon finally stood, and the teacher shifted aside, his face averted, as the surgeon walked to the door. By the time he opened it, the pharmacist had already turned and was running to the back room. 'Baba, baba,' the boy called as well, and at that sound the teacher rose from his crouched position and followed them.

In the middle of the back room was the teacher's wife, seated with her legs folded under her. The tube in her neck was perfectly still. Her son was kneeling behind her, gripping the side of her arm and pressing his lips into the back of her shoulder. Their eyes were trained on the swaddling of green cloth in her lap. Then the bundle twitched, and the pharmacist fell to her haunches, joined her hands in front of her face, and started to rock back and forth.

There was a second twitch, and a third. Even though the surgeon could see each one, it took him some time to realize what was – what could be – happening. The woman raised the bundle to him unopened, as though he were a deity to whom she were surrendering an offering. He knelt and took it from her, placed it on the mattress between them, opened it.

The infant had her arms held up against the sides of her body, bent at the elbows, the fingers with their soft nails curling and straightening in slow grasps at the air. The plump wrists creased, and the feet with their splayed toes kicked away at the fold of the drape in which they were entangled. The eyelids opened, and under them swam large black irises. The lips exposed toothless gums – as smooth as those of an old woman, the surgeon thought, and then realized that the comparison ought to be the other way around. It didn't matter, really – for whatever reason, life started and ended with the mouth polished of all its weapons. It was just the period in between that made everything so complicated. The baby was still blue – cool to the touch. The surgeon placed his palm on the newborn's chest and curled his fingers around the ribcage. The chest, delicate as it was, rose against his skin.

'Get my stethoscope.'

Someone placed it in his outstretched hand, and he ordered them all to be quiet. Too many people were saying too many things, the boy loudest of them all. The surgeon bent over the baby and moved the bell over her chest. The hard plastic earpieces pressed a dull pain into the sides of his head, and a low, quick beat sounded in them now that all other sounds had been silenced. But that wasn't the infant, no, it was just the beat of his own blood pulsing in his skull. He listened, and when he was convinced he'd listened enough, he peeled the stethoscope from his ears.

'She isn't...' he began, his eyes brimming, but found he couldn't bring himself to add the word *alive* to the end of that sentence. If this baby, who was stretching her limbs on the green cloth, whose ribs rippled under her dusky skin as she breathed and moved ... if such an infant wasn't alive merely for want of a heartbeat, then it was language and its prejudices that needed remedy. The infant's eyes were calm, almost solemn, with a slight wrinkle in the skin between them that gave her an expression of deep thought, as though she were indeed some ancient soul reborn, inspecting the world and its inhabitants for the last time before fully assuming the guise of a child.

'She isn't crying,' the surgeon said, unable to draw his gaze away from the infant, 'because she doesn't have any hunger or thirst or pain. Or fear. You've given birth to what might be the first creature on earth to ever know peace, because she needs nothing from this world.'

He then raised his eyes, and moved to hand the infant back to her mother. But the woman and her son were no longer kneeling on the floor before him. He jerked his head to where the teacher had stood, and found no one there either. In his haste to stand, he almost tripped over the infant, and had to balance himself on both palms to keep from falling on her. Raising himself would require more strength than he could summon, and so he twisted and slumped back down, this time facing the door, with the side of his hip and thigh against the floor and his torso propped up on the mattress by a forearm. The baby remained nestled within the arc of his body. Apart from the two of them, only the pharmacist and her husband remained in the room. She was still rocking on her haunches, her awestruck eyes darting between the infant and the surgeon, her palms joined before her lips as she breathed loudly in rhythm with her rocking. Her husband, on the other hand, seemed barely to breathe. He sat with his back against the doorjamb and his hands balled before him, as if braced against some invisible foe who might try to strike him from the air.

Seventeen

The surgeon checked every room of the clinic, and checked again. He tried a different sequence of rooms each time, as if it were possible for an entire family to play hide-and-seek with him in a place this small, and in broad daylight. The dead had vanished. All except the infant. The parts of the dead he'd extracted through the night – those were still in trays in the operating room. The things he'd attached to their bodies – the tubes and bottle and surgical dressing – had gone with them.

After his fourth circuit of the clinic, when it was clear that nothing more would be gained by his aimless wandering, the surgeon sat in the chair in his consultation room. This had to be the doing of the official from the afterlife. Perhaps he had realized that none of the three would survive their surgeries, and had pulled them back to spare them another death.

But why take them all back? The boy would have lived. His spleen was out. His wound wasn't bad. Why not give him a chance? Perhaps the official just couldn't make dead blood flow. Dawn had come and gone, after all, and nothing had happened. Who knew what other warnings from the official the teacher had ignored in his haste to regain life? The official, if he had any intelligence at all, must have had a plan for exactly such a scenario. If he couldn't make their blood flow, he wouldn't just leave the dead stranded in the middle of a village, waiting for someone to stumble upon the truth. Or for a surgeon to devise a monstrous scheme to bury their corpses.

But why leave the bloodless infant behind?

And what if this weren't the doing of the teacher's official? What if other officials were involved? Perhaps the teacher's official, the benevolent one, had been working away in the afterlife, hammering the gears of his plan into motion, restoring movement to the infant as the first step of his grand resurrection, when others discovered his plot. Perhaps they immediately pulled back the three people he had sent, without realizing that portions of their bodies had been left behind.

The surgeon realized that the clicking sound he was hearing was the tips of his incisors striking each other as they slipped over the smooth edge of his thumbnail. He placed his hands before him on the table, and watched his fingers quiver against the glass. Was he even permitted to think about the afterlife and its officials? Perhaps the officials could read thoughts, and were spying on him this very moment. If he chanced upon the right explanation for all of this, would they consider him too much of a risk and snatch him up?

And in the midst of all this was the awful feeling of relief that the dead were gone. They were no longer his problem, he wasn't responsible for them any more. At this thought, the surgeon pounded a fist on the table, making a pen on the edge rattle and fall off. What kind of person was he, to think like this? To have thought all those appalling things? What kind of selfish beast—

'Saheb?'

The pharmacist and her husband were standing in the doorway of his consultation room, at the precise spot where he had first seen the dead. They looked strange, but then so did everything else. The surgeon felt an urge to confirm their pulse.

'Don't ask me what's going on. Just ... *don't* ask me,' he said, rising from his chair and walking to the window. A glare of sunlight fell on his face, and he used the excuse to cover his eyes.

~

When the surgeon told the pharmacist and her husband to return to their home, the man looked relieved, but his wife pulled him aside. They argued in whispers outside the clinic for some time and then entered, having resolved their disagreement, one could say, though she did most of the talking while he stood by her side in glum silence. They couldn't leave Saheb here like this, she said. He was tired. Who knew what would happen next? It wasn't right that he should be alone. And if some calamity were to strike them, they wanted him to be around when it did. Besides, it was best if they didn't try to walk home in broad daylight. The neighbours would take one look at them and realize that something was wrong. And the baby, even if she weren't a child like every other, needed a woman to look after her.

The pharmacist's husband looked subdued – too tired to argue any further. It was clear that he was struggling with his wife's resolve.

The surgeon asked for a few minutes to think. The pharmacist went to the back room to check on the baby, while her husband followed her and stood with a listless expression outside the door. Then they both returned and waited for him to speak, forcing him to come up with a plan.

'We'll make the clinic look like it's closed,' the surgeon said. 'Like when we go to the city for supplies. Hopefully the villagers will see the shutters and not disturb us. It'll allow us to get some rest. My head feels like it's packed with rocks, but after I've had some sleep, I'll decide how we should keep the baby hidden.' He wanted to add 'until she vanishes as well', but realized that would be unnecessarily cruel, especially in front of the pharmacist.

At the surgeon's instructions, the pharmacist's husband went from window to window, securing each one from the inside. A few of the latches were broken, and he had to tie their handles together with rope. Almost all of the windows were made entirely of wood, and the ones in the operating room were of frosted glass, opaque from the outside.

The clots, the spleen, the placenta, all had to be disposed of before the heat and flies could start acting on them. The dead themselves had shown no evidence of decay while they were here, but who knew if their entrails would retain this immortality once separated from their bodies? The pharmacist ladled everything into plastic bags and, with the surgeon, carried them to the compost ditch. The sight of them puttering outside the clinic was familiar enough to the village for no one to give them a second thought. Nonetheless, as the surgeon emptied the bags into the hole, he could feel the muscles in his shoulders tense. It was deeply unpleasant, this feeling that he was disposing of evidence. He imagined everyone in the village stopping their work to look up at the hillock and memorize his every move. It reminded him also of the horrible thoughts he'd allowed himself to think. But there really was no other option. There were just two ways of doing this – fire or earth. It was no different from when the bodies of entire humans were bid farewell – either you sent up corkscrews of smoke to announce it to the heavens, or you chose the discreet path.

They packed enough soil over the ditch to prevent stray dogs from digging up its contents, and returned to the clinic. The pharmacist's husband closed the front door, placed a padlock on the outside, and climbed in through the small window where the pharmacist usually sat – the only window in the whole place without metal bars across it. He shut it from the inside, and the surgeon switched off the lights. Enough sunlight filtered through the cracks in the wood for them to see each other.

~

The pharmacist had peeled her blood-covered gloves off into the pit and, once back in the clinic, scrubbed her hands with soap until they were raw. Drying her hands on her dress, she walked to the back room. The baby was still on the mattress, as Saheb had left her. Her skin still blue and her face still calm, she was kicking her legs in the folds of the green drape tangled around them. The pharmacist brought her face close to the baby's and took a deep breath, but the infant gave off no smell. She tickled the baby's ribs and feet, but there was no response. The eyes were open, and the pharmacist moved her face back and forth in front of them. With the windows closed, the room was dark and, though the baby's eyes wandered, occasionally seeming to cross, it wasn't clear that she could truly see her. The pharmacist was struck by how seldom the baby blinked, and she realized that she'd never before seen a newborn this awake, one without a hint of drowsiness. She gathered the infant up in the drape, rested the head in the crook of her elbow, and held the scalp against her lips. After kissing it a few times, she placed the baby in the crib she had fashioned, and left the room.

At the far end of the pharmacy, she pulled out a sack of rice from beneath the stone platform. She pumped the stove to a high flame, set a pot of water on it, and added three cups of rice. While the water came to a boil, she picked around in a basket of vegetables for any still fresh enough to eat. Two potatoes, an onion, a few small tomatoes, a packet of legumes, an inch of ginger – it wasn't enough to make a single decent dish, so she just chopped them all up together. When the rice had softened, she took the pot off the flame and replaced it with a skillet. The tablespoon of oil she poured in took very little time to start rippling from the heat, and she added mustard and cumin and turmeric, let them crackle on the fire.

She thought of the boy, and the prison he had carved out of the thermocol box. She would never see him again, she knew that now, and she felt a rush of sorrow. She hoped he was at peace, and cared for, wherever he was. She hoped he was with his parents.

She added the chopped vegetables to the skillet, and the hot oil sent up its fumes, making her cough. After draining the excess water from the rice, she swept it into the mix and covered it with a lid. A sound behind her made her turn. It was her husband, carrying the supplies from the corridor into the pharmacy and arranging them on shelves. She caught his eye, and he stopped. He looked morose, but she knew it wasn't the moroseness of someone forced to act against his will. It was the anxiety of someone afraid of false hope. Hope had been unkind to them in their young marriage. He placed a hand on her shoulder, and she rested her cheek against it. Then the skillet spluttered, and she returned to it, and her husband to his boxes.

The pharmacist hadn't mentioned it to Saheb – he didn't believe in this kind of thing – and even her own husband, normally a pious man, thought she was losing her mind, but she knew this was no ordinary baby. It was an incarnation of some goddess. Her husband and she were blessed to have been chosen for this task. It all made sense to her now – why it had happened to them, why the dead had come to this world. It was to deliver this child into their care. Difficult as things seemed now, wasn't Krishna himself born in a prison cell on a night filled with bad omens – storms and a flooded river, and everything else? And look what greatness He was destined to achieve. If she did everything in her power to protect this child, raised her, devoted her life to her, who could say what miracles the child would perform, what evils and injustices she would drive from this world?

The pharmacist ladled the rice out into two plates. She wasn't feeling very hungry herself. The cramp low in her belly nauseated her. It wasn't her time of the month yet, so perhaps this was just from the scars left after the tuberculosis in her ovaries had closed off her tubes. Saheb was sure that all those months of antibiotics had been enough to cure the infection itself, and he always insisted that the scars, though they would probably never go away, shouldn't cause her pain. But what could you do? You accepted what God decided for you without asking too many questions. After all, if He could make this world and everything in it, put in its place every star in the sky and pebble in the river, then He understood the path laid out for you, life after life, better than any human ever would.

She carried the plates out.

~

Though the pharmacist kept apologizing for the tastelessness of the food, the surgeon barely stopped to chew as he swallowed. The same was true of the pharmacist's husband, who ate cross-legged on the floor. After the plates were cleared, the surgeon remembered the packets from the blood bank, and he transferred them from the icebox to the refrigerator. Perhaps another farmer with a lacerated forearm would walk in one of these days, and he'd have a chance to use them.

He waited in the corridor while the pharmacist laid out the makeshift beds. She had spread out two thin ones in the pharmacy, and now seemed to be arranging the one in his consultation room to be as comfortable as possible. They hadn't had to discuss it, but it was obvious that none of them had any desire to sleep in the back room, on any of the beds or mattresses that the dead had occupied.

'We're like kites,' said the surgeon.

'Kites, Saheb?' asked the pharmacist's husband.

'Yes. Kites with strings.'

To relieve a crick in his neck, the surgeon turned his face upward until he felt a pleasant squeeze in the flesh at the back of his scalp. He found, to his bemusement, the pharmacist's husband mirroring the action, turning to the ceiling as if in search of kites.

'You have to wonder,' said the surgeon, 'what a kite would think if it had a brain. Maybe it would think of its position in the sky as the only steady point in the universe, and worry about constantly holding the rest of the world in place. That, too, on a single string. A single string, at the end of which is balanced the entire earth, as if on the tip of a pin. The earth has so many dangerous things on it, trees with branches like claws, constantly trying to poke holes through the kite's body, animals crawling all over, waiting to grab and tear it, and water, so much water everywhere – the kite has to make sure it never touches it, or it will be done for. The wind is strong, it makes the earth flap around the kite in every direction, but the kite holds on to its string, keeps the earth at a safe distance. There's sin and death and evil on the earth, the kite thinks, but the sky is pure, and as long as it controls its own little patch, things are good.'

This seemed to perplex the pharmacist's husband. The surgeon waved a hand, dismissing the train of thought.

'Get some rest. Both of you. We'll talk again after we've slept.'

The pharmacist brought the crib from the back room and positioned it beside her bedding in the pharmacy. The surgeon knelt at its side, examining the baby again to confirm that she was still in her placid, bloodless state. He caressed her cheek with the back of a finger.

'If only this were a normal child, we could pretend that she was abandoned at our doorstep. Now, we'll have to just hide her. After it's dark, we can move her to my quarters, where no one will wander, and you can look after her there. Let's see how long we can keep this secret.'

The surgeon dragged himself to the consultation room and closed the door. His eyes, of their own will, went to the side table, to the teacup that the official's lips had touched. He gave it a long, quiet look, and thought of the teacher and his wife and son, of the place to which they had likely returned. He remembered what the dead woman had said, that the afterlife wasn't as bad as her husband made it out. He hoped that those words, uttered though they were in a fit of rage, were true. Somehow the prospect of the afterlife seemed to cause the surgeon less distress than he felt it should. Perhaps if he were less drained, the ghastliness of it might have overwhelmed him. But now, in this little room, surrounded by the apparatus of this mortal world, one of which was a prepared bed, the afterlife seemed like a distant calamity, to be confronted at a later, mercifully unspecified, date.

He thought of his last conversation with the teacher, of how wretched the man had looked, kneeling on the floor. He recalled how harsh he'd been with him, how needlessly bitter and cruel their final moments together had been. What would *he* have done in the teacher's place? Refused the possibility of life? Far greater men had sinned for far less. One thing the surgeon knew: the remorse he now felt would remain with him as long as he lived. And perhaps beyond.

He thought also of the bundle of money, a good portion of his savings, that he'd handed over to the official. At that last thought, he pulled an old handkerchief from a drawer, spread it out on his desk, placed the cup in its centre, and knotted the ends of the square to fold it into a bundle. He pinched the knots in his fingers, raised the bundle to the level of his eyes, and released it.

The smash was muffled, but apparently still loud enough to carry to the other rooms, for the pharmacist called out, 'Saheb?'

'Don't worry,' he said. 'I dropped something in the dark. I'll take care of it.'

An irresistible drowsiness overcame him. He lay down on the sheets without bothering to throw the handkerchief and its enclosed shards into the wastebasket. He had wondered if he would be able to sleep under the weight of everything that had passed, but as soon as his head touched the pillow, his eyes were sealed as though with a kohl of wax. His chest rose and fell. That wasn't a definite sign of life, of course. Only the few drops of sweat that pushed through his pores and trickled down his skin spoke of his persistence in this world.

The living slept as though death itself had scoured all thought from their minds. The clinic readied its bricks and mortar and settled into the silence of a tomb. In the corridor, a small green lizard, emboldened by the quiet, emerged from a crack in the ceiling and resumed its vigil beside the wall clock. Hours passed, marked by nothing more than the crawl of the clock's hands and the occasional dart of the lizard's flat tongue, until, in a box lined with cloth, by the side of a new mother deep in dreamless sleep, the slightest shade of pink crept into the cheeks of a newborn. Her fists balled, her face crinkled as she shut her eyelids tight, and her lips pulled back from her toothless gums while she drew in a breath, preparing to let out a cry.

Acknowledgements

Thank you to my editors: Peter Gelfan for helping this story find its direction, and Miranda Ottewell for helping it find its voice. Thank you to my agent Neil Olson for his dedication and insight. My gratitude to Nate, Shruti, Shalaka, Christine, Chris, Adam, Dhruv, Gouri, Tom, Thomas and Bruce for valuable conversations and comments, and to my parents for enveloping my childhood in books.

25 HarperCollins India Ltd

Celebrating 25 Years of Great Publishing

HarperCollins India celebrates its twenty-fifth anniversary in 2017. Twenty-five years of publishing India's finest writers and some of its most memorable books – those you cannot put down; ones you want to finish reading yet don't want to end; works you can read over and over again only to fall deeper in love with.

Through the years, we have published writers from the Indian subcontinent, and across the globe, including Aravind Adiga, Kiran Nagarkar, Amitav Ghosh, Jhumpa Lahiri, Manu Joseph, Anuja Chauhan, Upamanyu Chatterjee, A.P.J. Abdul Kalam, Shekhar Gupta, M.J. Akbar, Satyajit Ray, Gulzar, Surender Mohan Pathak and Anita Nair, amongst others, with approximately 200 new books every year and an active print and digital catalogue of more than 1,000 titles, across ten imprints. Publishing works of various genres including literary fiction, poetry, mind body spirit, commercial fiction, journalism, business, self-help, cinema, biographies – all with attention to quality, of the manuscript and the finished product – it comes as no surprise that we have won every major literary award including the Man Booker Prize, the Sahitya Akademi Award, the DSC Prize, the Hindu Literary Prize, the MAMI Award for Best Writing on Cinema, the National Award for Best Book on Cinema, the Crossword Book Award, and the Publisher of the Year, twice, at Publishing Next in Goa and, in 2016, at Tata Literature Live, Mumbai.

We credit our success to the people who make us who we are, and will be celebrating this anniversary with: our authors, retailers, partners, readers and colleagues at HarperCollins India. Over the years, a firm belief in our promise and our passion to deliver only the very best of the printed word has helped us become one of India's finest in publishing. Every day we endeavour to deliver bigger and better – for you.

Thank you for your continued support and patronage.